THE WILLOW TREE

THE FRAGMENT TRILOGY · PART ONE

Britain's Next
BESTSELLER

First published in 2015 by:

Britain's Next Bestseller
An imprint of Live It Publishing
27 Old Gloucester Road
London, United Kingdom.
WC1N 3AX

www.britainsnextbestseller.co.uk

ISBN 978-1-906954-37-6 (pbk)

This book is dedicated to the memories of
Margaret Ann Pate, Jean and John Mulholland,
Jean Hoggart and Mikey Dawson.

You are missed.

ACKNOWLEDGEMENTS

There are so many people that I wish to thank for helping me on this journey! Firstly, to Nick Denyer, who read and re-read the story, pointing out obvious flaws that I had missed, and offering honest feedback. Also to Sherrie Wright, who has supported my writing for years, whose opinion I value so much.

I would also like to thank those who helped with my campaign, who shared my endless posts and updates, who pestered their work colleagues and friends, who kept supporting me throughout: Robyn and Andy Mitchell, Lynn Shaw, Neil and Cath Denyer, Alice Priday, Joe Hall, Louise Burgum, Mary Wood, Becky A'Court-Turner, Sammy Pate, and others who kept me motivated!

Thank you so much to Britain's Next Bestseller for this amazing opportunity! I think this is the way forward for book publishing. Thank you to my fellow BNBS authors who have been hugely supportive and informative when I have asked silly questions about the process!

And thank you to those who have pre-ordered, you don't realise how much this means to me, how much I have wanted to simply become a published author, so I can leave something behind, to say that I have written something that people will read.

So that's it guys! Make some tea, find a quiet room, and enjoy!

FRAGMENT TRILOGY SUPPORTER LIST

Lynn Shaw, R. Mitchell, Nick Denyer, Sally Barber, Sherrie Wright, Samantha Pate, Nikki Kelly, Kate Chackett, Matt Bennett, Duncan and Leonie Wood, Lucy Dykes, Fabienne Schiess, Joe Hall, A Mitchell, Natalie, Rebecca Turner, Tarell Baker, Lou Burgum, Kayleigh Pennell, Ryan Toal, David East, Katie Louise Tate, Carli Bosworth, Linda Stokes, Kathryn Hall, Sophie Woods, Annie Woods, Stacey Stocks, Tracey Parker, Claire Vipond, Karen Lloyd, Alice Priday, Michelle Rouse, Lisa Daykin, Stephen Taft, Lucy Reynolds, Amy Lawson, Sharon Kempson, Laura Heysmond, Lin Tristam, Jayne Rankin, Donna Butler, Stella Metherell, Lauren Spencer, Gemma Liddicoat, Lisa Stacey-Brown, Georgie Sweeney, Alex Meredith, Marie Green, Joyce Ward, Teresa Byrne, Diane Whistance-Smith, Reneé Harper, Liz Radford, Ann Lloyd, Emma Virgilio, Jamie Radford, Andrew Smith, Donna Walker-McIntosh, Lucia (Wild Blood in my Veins), John Pate, Stacey Wall, Jane Husslebee, Jennie Yeomans, Julie Anderson, Rose Bell, Julie Icke, Linda Smith, Lou Farrer, Catherine Thomas, Rachel Sennett, Vanessa Hall, Val Clynes, Lin Roberts, Jo Ridley, April Chalotra, Lesley Wright, Joan Burnet, Karen Dugmore, Cath Denyer, Neil Denyer, Amy Denyer, Joyce Mason, Paula Foster, Ailsa Rowe, Katie Kochanowski, Ben Powell, Lesley Murphy, Tayla Ashley Clelland, Sean Starbuck, David McCaffrey, J.E. Plemons, Megan Jones, Chris Kirk, Emma Sharman, Claire Lomas, Chris Chackett, Kara Groome, Beth Rigby, Lucy Owen, Rachel Worcester, Goodchilds Bloxwich Ltd, Shirley Spencer Brown, Kate Hayes, Zoe Bamford, Sharon Bamford, Kelly Papanarva, Travis West, Aden Woods, Kyle Insley,

James Clark, Dan Lovely, Solomon Dantés, Simon Gibbs, Nicholas Green, Marky B, Julie Haines, Margaret Pate, Chloe Spruce, Sarah Penny, Ezekiel Frazer Chester, Ken Shaw, Emily Woodford, Sarah Cannon, Chloe Birley, Lizz Birley, Christopher Birley, Jake Jeffries, Ella King, Tracey aka Mrs Jingles, Saoirse Comstock, Michael Mccrackle, Jessica Colclough, Andrew Wood, Philip Mulholland, John Mulholland, Mary Wood, Marnie Fassett, Sandra Marshall.

Mark

Don't give yourself away. Pick up that blue brick over there. Now put it on the castle, it's going to be the turret. Keep focused, you can do this. Don't let him know, don't let him know.

I tried to keep focused on building my castle, but the weird man in the corner of the room kept looking at me. He was pale, white, and he smiled but it wasn't a nice smile. He showed too much teeth, and his eyes were too wide as they stared.

The man then started to move, shuffling along the floor towards me. He was now kneeling forwards, his hands flat against the floor, inches away from my face. Tears fell from my eyes, but I didn't want to cry; I didn't want him to know how scared I was.

I flinched when he reached out and touched me with his cold, greasy hand, his fingers brushing past my flushed face. But I couldn't scream for Mum and Dad; they couldn't help.

Nicky was in the corner, crying, whimpering. My baby brother, only five years old and this horrible man had tried to grab him and take him away. But I stopped him, and I told him that it was me he wanted, it was me with the powers. Of course it was, because I was ten and I knew how to work my powers. What would a five year old need to be able to see into the future for?

Of course, it made sense, I just hoped that he didn't figure out I was lying.

"Don't worry Nicky," I said, but I kept my eyes on the man. "Its going to be alright."

A memory flashed through my mind then. When Nicky was first brought home, I didn't like him; I wanted them to take him back. But I was told that this wasn't allowed.

I remember sulking for a while, until Dad sat me down and told me that this purply, gross-looking thing was my brother, and that he loved me, and that I should take care of him.

And I have ever since.

If this man thought he would be leaving my house with my brother, he could bloody well think again, as my Dad sometimes said.

The man asked me again if I was lying. His breath was disgusting, and his mouth was dry and cracked. I shook my head, wiping away more tears. I held my head up high, sticking out my chin in defiance.

He told me that I could never come back. Nicky then ran to me, and wrapped his arms around my legs. He cried for me not to go, but I pushed his arms away and knelt down. I gave him a hug, something I never usually did, and I told him to go and get Mum, who was downstairs in the living room with Dad. Nicky was still for a while, looking at me, confused. He frowned at the man before looking back at me.

"Go," I repeated. "Now. Go." I gave him a little shove, and he went slowly towards the bedroom door. I heard him run down the stairs.

I turned to the man, my fear gone.

"You had better do it now then, before they come back."

The man studied me for a few seconds, making up his mind.

In the end, he believed me. In the end, he took me away, and I went with a smile, knowing that I had saved my little brother.

2

Aria

I heard the snap of their jaws, the click and scrape of their fingernails on the cold, metal door. They were angry, impatient, hungry. Their loud, tortured screams pierced the otherwise quiet corridor; there was no one left now. No one left, except me.

A sob caught in my throat, but I balled my fists up tight; I couldn't be so pathetic as to cry now. I had to be ready, prepared to fight, when they eventually broke down the door.

Looking back at Laura, her body now cold, I saw that her blue eyes were open, looking at me, her golden hair cradling her head, her broken neck. It gave me fire, hatred, anger, what I needed. It fed my desire to kill.

But I just needed to hold onto myself, before I forgot everything that I was supposed to be here for. It wouldn't be long, I could already feel the haze growing around me.

A bang lifted me from my thoughts, brought my heart leaping into my throat. They scratched and punched the door, and I watched in horror as it began to give way. I shuffled back to the dark corners of the room in terror as a long, bony hand started feeling around for the lock. Another punch, another slimy hand. A milky eye. A sharp, lapping tongue. I felt sick.

The haze kept growing, kept distracting me. *Don't lose yourself, don't. You're Jenny, you're Jenny, your mother is dead beside you. If*

3

you remember nothing else, remember that. I know who I am, I know who I am, I...know...I...

...A dream, that's all this was, a stupid, harmless nightmare. Or had I just woken up from one? *Where am I? What's that noise?*

I opened my eyes to find tears streaming down my face, my head banging, my fingernails black. *What the fuck?!*

I looked at the hands that were attached to my arms, attached to me, and they were those of a stranger. The lines...so unfamiliar, the marks and freckles, foreign to me.

I looked around. The room was dim, but not completely dark. It was quite bare, save for a few tables and chairs. There was a single, dirty window, where the moon shone brightly through. And underneath that, was a body.

I screamed, I didn't mean to, but I did, and that was when I heard a horrific roar. My eyes were pulled away from the poor woman who was staring at me intently as though she was still alive, and they rested on the door in front of me.

Dozens of eyes stared back at me through various holes, and a collective low growl made the room vibrate. The eyes were white, completely, like someone had placed a kind of skin or film over them. They were placed quite hollowly into sharp, bony faces. There were chattering teeth and overhanging jaws.

Fingers reached for the lock, scraping an arm through a small, jagged hole in the door. The metal drew blood, a blue, oozing fluid that dripped. But the creature did not notice. The key was turned, it clicked, and the door swung open.

All I could do was stare back at them, my limbs heavy and slow from terror. The creatures were tall, some were stood, looming over me, some were crouched, like animals, waiting to pounce. I let out a choked cry, and tried to burrow deeper into the corner.

A couple of them noticed the dead woman, sniffed the air, and crawled over to where she lay. They smelled her hair and licked her skin, and then proceeded to tear off her clothes.

"No!" I tried to shout. "Stop!" But my voice came out as little more than a squeak. *What good would it do anyway?*

I clasped my hand over my mouth to stifle another scream. They were tearing at her flesh now, pulling her skin away from her muscles, and dropping it delicately into their mouths. One took her pale, cold arm, and tore it from her body with a sickening crack. The creature clamped its mouth over the flesh and bone, and crunched its way through the meat.

I'm sorry, you poor woman, I am so sorry I can't save you. My only consolation is that you are already dead. I need to run...get up, get out of here! For fuck's sake you're going to be next. Run! Run! RUN!

I stood up, and faced the rest of the creatures, who were still blocking the door. They approached me, sniffing me through the air, and turning their long necks to scope out the rest of the room before turning their attention back to me. When they were almost upon me, I darted to the left, banging into a table. But I wasn't stopping for anything, let alone a sudden searing pain in my leg, so I half ran, half crawled, out of the room.

Sharp nails tugged at my skin, and hot, stale breath, wet with human blood, prickled the back of my neck. I ran down a small, narrow corridor, the sterile whiteness hurting my eyes, but they were inches behind me.

I kept running.

At the end of the corridor I found another door. I came to it so fast that I almost fell through it, but I yanked it open and slammed it behind me just in time. The creatures were so close that as I closed the door, they bashed into it, creating a series of yelps and shrieks from them. I locked the door, knowing it would only buy me mere seconds.

This room was larger, with more windows, and I ran to the nearest one to open it, hopping over the half eaten bodies that littered the floor. Whoever these creatures were, they'd had fun here, they'd had a feast, and some of these bodies, ripped open and with the insides devoured, were of children.

I need to get out of here.

The door behind me was flung open, and I screamed again as they scurried and leapt towards me.

The windows would take too long to open, so I ran for another door at the end of the room. I reached for the door knob and twisted it. It was locked.

This cannot be happening! I'm going to die! I'm going to be eaten by these disgusting things! Oh God!

There was only one option. I turned around and faced them, my heart pounding thunderously in my chest. My wide, tired, horrified eyes met their milky stares. There was one, taller than the others, who stepped forward, a sickly smirk on his face, a low, guttural chuckle escaping his lips.

This is it; I'm dead, and I don't even know what I'm doing here.

I closed my eyes, and waited for one of them to grab me, to claw and scratch at me. *Will they kill me first and then eat me? Or eat me alive? Where would they start? Will anyone ever find my remains?*

A loud smash broke my soft sobbing, and I opened my eyes in fright. A dark form had erupted through one of the windows in the musty room. It was long, like a snake, but sturdier, more rough. Another one broke a second window, and others followed it. The creatures turned in surprise, and didn't have time to utter a sound before swarms of these things surrounded them, and wrapped around their limbs. The creatures were torn apart, torn inside out. I could smell a familiar earthy smell, and it was only when one of the limbs brushed against my skin, that I realised what they were. Tree branches.

The branches forced themselves into the creatures' throats, and down, choking them, and ripped them from the inside out. I looked away to save the horrific memories, but I could still hear the rip and tear of skin, the wet smack of snapped bones, the gurgles coming from the creatures as they were unable to say much more.

An eerie silence followed, and I forced myself to open my eyes. There was nothing left except twitching body parts and blue, oozing fluid. The branches slithered back out the windows. When I had regained my ability to move, the only sound in the room was my deafening short gasps for air.

I nearly died tonight. I was nearly killed. Everyone else was killed.

Where the fuck am I?

I moved quickly, the need to put as much space between myself and this hell hole almost making me sick. I punched through one of the windows, cutting my hand. I dragged my aching body out of the building, and into the fresh air.

I then ran, I ran through numerous fields until I found a road. I walked down the road, sobbing, until I could no longer walk. After that I don't remember much, except curling up beside the road, freezing, the only warm thing on my body were my tears. I was losing consciousness. And a car…I remember a car…and footsteps, coming towards me.

CHAPTER TWO
SPRING, 1852

Freya

As I looked up towards the bright blue sky, I could see the trees swaying majestically in the breeze all around me. I reached out my hand and touched one of the green leaves, lightly, and it sent a warm shudder through my body. I could smell the earth, and I could feel the warm air circling me as I sat on my favourite tree stump.

I felt at peace here, in the woods near my house; it was the only place where I could think, and reflect. It was also the only place where I could be my true self, without submitting to ridicule from others, who would accuse me of dealing with the Devil or playing tricks on people's minds. It wasn't something I could describe with any accuracy; it was more of a feeling, a connection, to all things. As I sat there, reading quietly, as I usually did, I felt a sudden pull. I looked up, and saw nobody, but I knew it was not a person. This was a spirit of nature, calling for me to help it. I closed my book and set it down, and proceeded to follow the voice through the trees, whose own voices sung out as strong and as powerful as their sturdy branches.

I walked slowly to an opening in the woods, where the voice had led me to a small, withered tree. I knelt beside it, and I could immediately feel its pain. It was dying, but from what I did not know. It didn't matter, I had to heal it. I closed my eyes and emptied my mind of all other thoughts, and sought to find the green tendrils of energy that radiated from all the other living things around me. I took it, not by force, but because there was an abundance of it, it was everywhere, and I fed it into the dying tree. Almost at once I could hear it sigh in relief, I could feel its strength returning, its will to live becoming brighter.

After a few seconds, my task was complete, and I opened my eyes to find the small tree, which only a few moments ago had given up. It was now sprouting green, healthy buds, and I knew it would live for a long time.

In an otherwise solitary and painful life, my secret was the only thing that gave me strength, hope. I was a lonely, rather secretive sixteen-year-old girl with no friends. But then again, I rarely had a desire for them, although sometimes I wished that I could just fit in with other people. The girls I knew who lived near me never talked to me, and when they did, it was never to say anything nice.

My mother told me once that they were just jealous because I had been fortunate enough to be taught how to read and write, and they hadn't. I kept telling myself that, but deep down I knew it was just because they didn't like me. I would watch as they played in the sun, laughing and running around, or just sitting together and talking, and I could not help feeling jealous of them.

But still, I had my books, which were more precious to me than anything else in the world. I loved the tales and adventures of the characters and what they would get themselves into. I could escape with my books and pretend I was somewhere else, doing something important or going on an adventure. I could be anywhere but here. My mother once said I had a wild imagination and that I should use it to my advantage. That was when I started writing my stories. I used to show her them and she said they were the best she had ever read.

It was my Grandfather who taught my mother and me how to

read. He used to sit in his old wooden chair with a blanket wrapped around his legs, smoking his pipe and telling stories. He also used to tell me about what he used to get up to as a young boy, according to my mother, but I had long forgotten what he had told me about that. In fact, I thought to myself, the only intact memory I had left of him was when he used to sit in his chair. I think he may have been smiling. The rest was fuzzy and incomplete. We still had the old chair in the front room but his blanket had been misplaced years ago.

My father was working on our farm. We ate almost every meal from what he had grown and so we hardly ever went without food. My mother said that we are more fortunate than some families, who sometimes went days without meals. That was when I started noticing how plump I looked compared to the other girls. I seemed enormous next to their bony frames. That was probably another reason why they did not like me. It seemed, at one time, that my mother was the only friend I had. Sighing heavily, I thought about the talks and the fun she and I used to have together.

That all abruptly stopped as soon as my little brother was born. It seemed that I had become almost ghost-like since then; appearing and disappearing and no one would even notice. I would carry out my daily chores and sometimes help my father with his work without even so much as a thank you. I felt more like a maid flitting from room to room, tidying up and looking after everyone, rather than the child that I was. At the time, however, I was considered a grown up, and I was expected to act as such.

I remembered when my brother was born; I hated him. He cried and screamed almost every night for months, and all of my mother's attention was taken up by him. He had stolen her from me, and I resented him for it. She was with him all the time, and when she left him for just one second, he would kick and scream and

10

tantrum. They were together today, in fact, down by the lake. She was teaching him how to swim. It seemed pointless to me as he hated the water and would cry if he was even given a bath.

The lake itself was quite small, but clean and crystal clear. My mother used to take me swimming when I was younger, on lovely hot days like the one today, and I used to love it. I stopped going after he was born; it was too much hassle. He would make me so angry sometimes that it would reduce me to tears. His yells pierced the silent air at night, and I would wake up, alarmed for a second, not knowing who or what was making that terrifying, high-pitched shriek. Then I would realise and try endlessly to get back to sleep.

After a while I learned to block out his persistent, miserable whimpering and crying in the night. I saw that my anger towards him was pointless because he did not understand it and it was not going to make him go away. So it was repressed. This period of my life was when my books and stories became my safety nets. I used to go outside and sit in the garden, engrossing myself in the story, or, like I was today, go and sit in the small wooded area on my tree stump. So here I was, reading silently but passionately, the wind continuing to blow, but as the atmosphere was warm, almost clammy, I did not mind.

Some time later, I was disturbed from my story by a sound. I had just started the seventh chapter, and I was annoyed because after a long and drawn out introduction, the story had just started to gather speed. I looked up, and expected it to be one of the girls that were playing here earlier. I thought they might have been calling me names, but the more hopeful side of me thought that they might have been calling me over to join in with them. It was neither. It was a voice that I should have recognised straight away, and part of me did, I think. It was my mother.

"Freya! Freya!" she called. I could hear but not see her, and so I

11

turned the corner of the page where I had read up to in my book, and then closed it, glancing over the cover once more before I stood up. It was dark green, but blank, apart from the words 'The Treasure' written on it with gold lettering. My fingers trailed over the first 'T'. It had been sown in somehow.

I stood up, rearranging my skirts and brushing my hair out of my face. The wind had turned colder, sharper. I walked towards my mother's voice, looking down as I stood on the crispy golden leaves. They made a satisfying crunch underneath me. Then I saw her. She was looking in my direction but she did not see me.

"I'm here mother!" I called to her, waving my arms in the air. I had a horrible feeling that she was going to ask me to go and start the dinner, or to go and help my father or to take my brother home.

She saw me, and I looked into her eyes with shock; I had never seen them so full of fear. I noticed she was soaking wet, and thought she might have accidentally fell into the lake with her skirts and shawl on.

I did have to take my brother home that day, but it wasn't how I expected. I took him from my mother, after persuading her to give him to me, as she looked like she would collapse. I noticed how blue his face looked. His purple lips were set shut, and his eyes were closed. He was wrapped up in my mother's pink shawl, curled up, tight. His skin seemed translucent next to it. I ran back to the house where my father was still working, with the tiny bundle in my arms, holding him tight to my chest, against my pounding heart. I was closely followed by my hysterical mother, who kept repeating the same sentence over and over.

"My baby, my poor baby," she whispered. My father however, when we reached him, was unable to help.

My little brother had drowned, small and helpless, in the lake. He was only two years old.

Nick

I could still feel the heat of the fire on my skin, the smell of burning bodies, the shrieks of terror that pierced the air. I tried to get as many people out as I could, away from the horror inside, but those...those things...they were so fast, so brutal, they slaughtered my friends in front of me, my co-workers, people I grew to love and know as my family. And now Laura wasn't returning my calls. Neither was Jenny.

Do I go back? Stay in Laura's living room? Search the streets in my car?

I grabbed my coat and went back outside, slamming the door shut. I couldn't just sit there. I had to find Jenny, I had to know she was safe.

I called the police when I first got into my car, and told them there had been a fire, but I couldn't stay to answer questions. I had too many of my own.

I drove slowly through the streets, peering into every darkened alley, every young girl's face, every house with windows open. Nothing.

I decided to drive back to the facility, I had to meet her on the way at some point, and if not...I would go in to retrieve the body.

The night was cold, rainy, but a nervous, terrified sweat kept me from feeling it. I feared the worst. I couldn't find her, it had been hours already. If she was alive she would have called me. There was no other explanation.

I saw the aura in the corner of my eye, and had just enough time to park up and switch off the engine before my vision hit me. A sharp stab to my temple like a hammer, and a flash, an image, was forced into my mind. Jenny, standing in the rain, cold, shivering, under a street lamp. She was confused, crying, searching for me. Another flash, the surrounding area, a street name. It was close. Another flash, then white. My vision faded.

I opened my eyes, blinked, and focused again on my steering wheel. My hands had been gripping it so tightly that my fingers had pins and needles, and my head had somehow slumped forwards onto it. The horn was going off…and a few people had stopped to see what was going on.

I wiped the drool off my chin and waved at them.

"I'm alright thanks!" I mouthed through the window. I gave them a thumbs up and smiled. They continued to stare as I drove hastily away. *Fucking nosy bastards.*

I sped all the way to where my vision had told me to go, and I found her there, under the street lamp, exactly where I knew she would be. *My Jenny, I have you back. Thank God.*

CHAPTER FOUR

Aria

Smoke, voices, chaos. The images in my mind overwhelmed me. I heard screams and shouting, and saw endless hallways. I felt like I was floating. The last thing I saw before I came hurtling back to consciousness was two very blue, cold, lifeless eyes. They were looking at me. I didn't like it.

I woke up, my hazy mind clearing. I could smell what I could only describe as something like disinfectant, with the undercurrent of cheap food, and I heard voices and saw lights flickering all around me underneath my eyelids.

There was a faint mumbling of people talking in hushed voices, and squeaky shoes on the floor. I heard the occasional cough and sneeze, and I felt warm air emanating from an open window. Birds were chirping outside, and cars drove past.

I tested my immediate surroundings with my fingertips, searching for clues. I felt the rough blanket that strapped me into place, and at the back of my head I felt a pillow. It was soft, yet it was at such an angle that I felt propped up, as if I were on show. My whole body was stiff, tight.

As I lay there pretending to still be asleep, a sense of dread washed over me, a kind of hopeless despair.

I was shocked that I could feel the suffering around me, and I smelt the sweet earthy smell of death. There was so much pain packed into such a small area, and for a few seconds it overwhelmed everything else I had been afraid of. But then, as quickly as those feelings entered my head, they were gone.

"Are you awake?"

The voice was male, rough, tired. I opened my eyes in terror as everything came flooding back to me. The creatures, the dead woman. *They ate her...* I sat up.

"Jesus Christ!" I yelled, my hand grasping the back of my neck. Pain shot through my spine, and I was forced to lay back down on the bed. My eyes flew over to the man sitting beside me. He looked at me in fright and concern.

"Oh my God, are you okay? Shall I get the doctor?" He went to stand up, brushing his dark hair out of his eyes. He was tall. *Like them; like the creatures.*

"Where am I? What's happened?" I asked him. "I need to get out of here!"

Hysteria rose in my throat, it tasted like burnt sugar.

What if the creatures find me? What if they are already here?

"Don't worry, calm down," the man said. "Beth!" he called over his shoulder. Then, turning back to me. "You're safe now, it's alright."

"But those monsters!" I cried. "They killed everyone!"

He looked at me, a peculiar look darkening his face. He thought I was mad, or concussed, or something. But I wasn't; I was perfectly sane, and I needed to get moving.

A young girl, a nurse, came running over to me. I heard him whisper something into her ear, but I didn't catch what was said. She frowned, and then fixed a smile onto her face as she came closer to me.

"Are you feeling okay?" she asked. "You must be quite confused – my friend here found you in the street. He brought you here. You're safe, don't worry."

16

"But the monsters!" I cried. *Okay, now that does sound nuts.*

"There aren't any monsters here, sweetie," she replied. "I'll just get the doctor for you."

"No!" I protested. "I need to go! I need to leave! Now!"

People had started to stare at me; other patients, visitors, nurses, but I didn't care. They didn't know what I knew. Unless…they were all in on it? What if these people were all working for the same cause? They would take me straight to those creatures.

I tried to get up again, but the pain in my neck and back was excruciating. Suddenly I couldn't breathe. Everything was a blur. I felt strong hands grab my arms and pin me down. It was Beth. She must be one of the creatures, she must be in disguise. I tried to take a swing at her, but more nurses appeared, a doctor, he had a needle in his hand. *No! I am not going to let this happen.*

Something rose inside me then, something that should have felt familiar to me, but it didn't. My skin hummed and a tingling energy began to move through my veins. Electricity prickled between my fingers. I had to get out, get away, and suddenly I knew how I was going to do it.

The energy had collected in my hands; bright, green, fierce. The nurses stopped what they were doing, Beth was staring at the green light in curiosity more than anything, but the others were scared. Everyone backed away from me.

"Get back," I warned. "Get back now, otherwise I'll throw this at you."

Everyone stepped back even further, one nurse had tears in her eyes. *Please don't cry, I'm not actually going to hurt anyone, I just need to get out of here.*

I stood up on the bed, shaking, my legs weak, and my eyes met those of the man who found me. He looked hurt, betrayed almost. *Don't take it personally; even* you *might be one of those things, how am I meant to know?*

I took an unsteady step forwards, then another, and then I ran out of the ward, darting aimlessly through the corridors, pushing past anyone who was in my way, and out of the hospital.

I kept running and running, stopping only for a few minutes when nausea forced me to, until I found an old park. I wasn't sure how long I had been running, but it had started raining, and it was growing dark. I could see a cemetery up ahead just past a group of swings and a slide. To the left was a clearing, and something in it so bright that I had to shield my eyes from it.

The energy, it was everywhere, in everything. How had I not seen it before? It was living, fluid, in myself, the grass, the air, even the rain. But what stood out, bright, old and oddly comforting, was a huge willow tree. I couldn't help but walk over to it, my fear suddenly gone.

"What is this?" I asked it, as though I expected it to answer. "What am I doing here? Why are these things after me?"

Hard, painful tears cut through my eyes, and stained my cheeks. The willow tree hummed with an old energy, wise and constant. I let out a sob, and leant against it, sinking down into the muddying grass. This was the closest I had felt to home all day.

It was only then that an awful, horrifying thought gripped me, and wouldn't let go. *I don't know who I am, I don't know my name. Who is my family? Where do I live?*

Clenching my fists together and bashing them against the ground, I suddenly realised I was helpless. I had nowhere to go. I let out a loud cry of defeat and grabbed at my own hair, tearing bits out. I wanted to just go away, to just disappear into nothing and never have to deal with anything ever again.

The willow tree tried to soothe me with its energy. I found myself clinging to it like a child would cling to its mother's legs, and I sobbed and sobbed until my voice became nothing more than a dry croak.

I felt the change in the willow tree before I heard a sound that was only magnified due to the terror I felt at that moment. A twig. Snapped by a walking foot.

I spun around in the darkness. I couldn't see anything. I tried to gather together some energy, the only thing I was sure of, but before I could even begin, I felt a slimy, wet, large fist punch me in the face. My head snapped back and I fell back against the tree.

I saw wet skin glistening in the dark, wetter from the rain, and I heard a snigger, deep and inhuman. I then heard another, from another direction. And another. They had surrounded me.

I gathered a ball of energy in my hands, it was bright, green, soothing, but it only served to light up the area around me, and I saw then over a dozen beady eyes that had caught the light of the ball. The energy dissipated with my resolve, and I screamed again as something grabbed my ankle.

Closing my eyes, I sunk even further into the tree, willing it to just pull me inside, so I wouldn't have to deal with the pain of being beaten to death and then eaten.

I heard a *whoosh!* sound, the snapping and groaning of branches, a yell, then I smelt dirt. Another sound, more snaps, I felt leaves brush against my face, almost whipping me, and shouts and cries. I lit another ball of energy, quickly getting used to how to use it, and I saw the battlefield before me.

The willow tree's roots had come up out of the ground, and pulled several creatures under. I saw what looked like mole hills but larger, and the odd arm sticking out, twitching. I looked up. Creatures were hanging from the tree branches, their long legs swaying with the final throws of their bodies before they suffocated. One creature was still struggling, and so a branch wrapped itself around its neck, and its head popped off like a bottle cork.

In the next instant, there was nothing left of them except a blue gunk that soon washed away with the rain.

The willow tree was then still. I grabbed my chest, trying to still my thundering heart. I heard a car pull up again, just outside the park, and two figures got out.

Beth, and the man.

I've been followed.

This time I would be ready, this time they wouldn't get anywhere near me. I gathered another ball, and waited for them to get close enough so I could throw it at them. They saw the light, and ran over to it.

"Hey!" I heard the man shout. "Stop!"

"We're here to help!" Beth cried.

No you're not; you think I'm that stupid?

"Fuck off!" I screamed. "Get away from me!"

I looked down at my hands. *No!* The ball of energy had disappeared. I formed another, and a branch of the willow tree swiped down at it, making it scatter as though it was dust in the air. I made another, purely to see what the willow would do this time, and it swiped again. *What?*

I looked back at the two figures.

"Hey! Sorry about what happened back there. It got kind of messy," Beth said.

"Who *are* you people?" I screeched. I held up my fists, ready for a fight. I couldn't see them properly in the darkness, but that also meant they couldn't see me.

"We're here to help, as I said," Beth continued.

"Yeah," added the man. "We saw what you did back there and…we understand. We can help."

"Please, please just leave me. I'm dangerous," I replied, beginning to sob again. I was exhausted, hungry, my head pounded and I could taste blood from where the creature had hit me. I then felt a rough, leafy branch place itself against my back. It gave me a shove forward, only a little one, but enough for me to go stumbling a few paces forwards. I tripped over a stone and landed in the man's arms.

"Woah! Steady, I've got you," he said. He lifted me up like a rag doll. "Stop struggling, we aren't going to hurt you. Look, my name is Ash, and this is Beth."

All I could do was whimper. Beth was beside him, and she pulled my matted hair out of my face. I heard her intake of breath.

"Jesus, Ash, she's hurt. We need to take her back to the flat," she said to him.

"Alright. Does that sound okay with you?" he said to me, like I was a child.

"We have a cup of tea with your name on it," Beth smiled.

"Or something stronger, you look like you need it."

And then, for the second time in one day, I was piled into a car, barely conscious, and driven away by a stranger.

CHAPTER FIVE

Freya

It was a cold day, and the sky heaved with unshed rain. I was sat under a large tree with my book unopened in my hands. I had been trying to concentrate on it for a while but my mind kept wandering, forcing me to relive the events that had been occurring over the past few months at my house.

My mother had been spiralling deeper and deeper into a sort of melancholy state. Her eyes had become dull and her movement slow. She looked old and haggard. It was painful to watch. She never even looked at me anymore, not even when I spoke. My father had remained unconvincingly optimistic throughout our ordeal, trying to cheer up my mother, but it never worked. She would never be the same.

As for me, I was more of a ghost now than I ever was before. I was left unseen; uncared for, my mother not even noticing when I had been out for hours on end. My father talked to me at the dinner table, but it was little more than pointless talk to maintain a normal exterior. I reassured myself that some day things would get better.

As I sat under the tree, I noticed that since my brother died, I have had a feeling in the pit of my stomach that I had never been able to identify until now. I felt guilt; I was guilty because I was sure that if I had been there, if I had seen what was happening, I could have called upon my secret to save my little brother from drowning.

Although even my secret was not what it once was; I could feel it almost slipping away, or perhaps more accurately, transforming into something else, something that scared me a little. I was changing it as recent events had changed me. The terrible thoughts that plagued me every day had affected my ability to connect to the earth, to feel the energy in everything, and to draw upon it to help others. It was becoming poisonous within me, but that was not the worst part. The worst part was that I let it manifest into something I could use for myself, for my own selfishness, and a part of me loved every second of it. It seemed better this way.

The girls appeared then, playing with their dog, who was a small, scabby looking creature with only one eye. One girl threw a stick, and the dog ran to fetch it, its expression rather dim-witted. I quickly opened my book, pretending not to hear their snide remarks upon seeing me. I saw the words on each page, but no matter how hard I concentrated, I was too distracted to take any of it in. A few moments passed, and after seeing that their comments did not have the effect they wanted it to, I looked up just in time to see a tree branch come hurtling towards me. I didn't however, have time to move before it hit me, hard, in the face.

I inhaled in shock and pain and brought my hand up to my cheek. I was bleeding; they had made me bleed. And all they did was laugh. Anger churned within me, enveloping me, and from somewhere deep inside an urge to scream was bubbling. I could almost hear it.

I glared at the girls, my eyes growing hot as I watched them laughing in the grass. I was so confused as to why and how they could treat me this way, even after knowing what I had been through. It wasn't fair, they had to learn...

I then turned my eyes away from the two girls and their scabby dog, and closed my book. My eyes became cool again, and the anger subsided a little, as it was overcome by embarrassment. I quickly stood up and briskly walked back to my house, staring at the ground. As I left the two girls behind, I clutched my cheek, and saw smears of blood on my hand as I brought it away again.

Hardly thinking, I balled up my fist and thrust it into the nearest tree. Images of my brother danced under my closed eyelids. He was naked and crying, curled up into a tiny ball, as cold as ice.

Shock brought me back to my senses seconds later.

I opened my eyes with a shudder, and to my horror, my fist was embedded inside the tree trunk. Imagining at least a broken finger, I winced as I pulled it out. It didn't hurt. Looking at my hand, and seeing that there was not one scratch on it, I studied the trunk of the tree, assuming that it must be old and rotten. But It was not; in fact it was a strong, robust tree, its energy pouring out from its branches and leaves and dripping into the ground, where it was absorbed again.

Then, the hole where I had punched through the trunk began to peel away, as if somebody was holding fire against it. The bark curled and blackened, and I stepped back as this blackness spread from the inside of the trunk out and onto the exterior bark. The branches withered and sagged, and the leaves turned brown and crumpled to the floor. It became a husk, empty and exposed.

I brought my hands up to my face as the tree died in front of me, its life force extinguished from just my mere thinking it. The only other thought that entered my mind then was how easy it had been, and how, for some agonising reason, I itched to do it again. Turning away from the tree, I ran home. There I found my mother staring hard into space, clutching her wrists that my father had only recently bandaged, fresh blood pouring from them once again.

CHAPTER SIX

Nick

Jenny's soft hair tickled my face, waking me up when all I wanted to do was spend a few more minutes asleep, before I had to deal with the police and make statements, possibly identify bodies. *Just let me sleep, let me laze in ignorance a little while longer.*

I rolled over, and half consciously felt Jenny get up and make her way to the bathroom. At least she was here, at least I had found her, and I could hold her and make her feel safe.

She had told me that Laura was dead, but apart from that she didn't really speak at all. It must have been the shock, the trauma of it all, getting to her. I would give her a few days to come to terms with her loss, and then we could figure out what exactly happened.

"Oh, for fuck's sake," I groaned, as the familiar aura, like a migraine, hit me with full force. Gripping the bed, I prepared myself. The images ripped into my mind's eye, sending shooting pains up the base of my neck. *Jenny.* She was sat in a café, sipping a hot drink. She had been crying, and her clothes were torn, dirty, her face bloody. A barista came over and gave her shoulder a reassuring squeeze, and she smiled sadly up at him. *What?* Another flash. My bathroom. Jenny was in there, but wait…her face…what *is* that?

I heaved my body up to vomit into the bucket I kept by my bed for such occasions. Sometimes my visions caused an awful sea-sick feeling, and I can't help but throw up.

25

After the pain and nausea had cleared, I wiped my face, my gaze fixed on the bathroom door. It was closed, water was running. I pulled out the cricket bat I kept behind Jenny's bed for the midnight intruders that always turned out to be the water pipes or the neighbours, and slowly advanced. Whatever was in Laura's house, it was an imposter, and my sweet Jenny was still out there somewhere.

"Hello?" I called. The girl didn't answer. *Who the fuck is she?* "Jenny? What are you doing in there sweetie?"

She opened the door, still completely naked, and my mind flashed back to the night before. We'd had sex. I'd had sex with someone who wasn't my girlfriend.

Her face fell as she noticed the cricket bat.

"Nick, what are you doing?" she asked.

"Who are you?" I whispered, my body shaking.

She blinked in confusion.

"What? It's me, Jenny."

"What's your last name then?"

"For God's sake, I'm not doing this…" She went to storm out of the room, but I brought the bat down hard against the wall next to her, making her stop in surprise and fright, the dull slap reverberating through the room.

"Your last name," I repeated.

"Bailey. I'm Jennifer Bailey. Now let me past," she huffed.

"What's my name?" I asked.

"Seriously?"

I glowered at her.

"Fine. Nicholas Jenkins. You're being a twat." She made to move again, but I blocked her path.

"How long have we been together?"

"Five years."

"How did we meet?"

"At the facility."

"Oh, you're good," I admitted. Someone must have briefed her on the basics. I needed something more personal. "Right, do you remember a few years ago when we had a picnic by the lake, and I asked you to marry me?" She nodded. "You refused. Tell me why."

I watched a flash of panic pass over her face. *I've got you now, you bitch.* She pretended to think about it for a few seconds.

"I can't quite recall, but was it because I wanted to focus on my career? I remember the proposal, but not quite why I said no. But that was so long ago sweetie, how am I supposed to remember everything? You were sweet though, maybe if you tried again, I might not say no this time. You know…"

I cut her rambling short with a blow to the head, as swift and as brutal as I could muster. It knocked her to the ground, and blood began to trickle from a gash on her temple. The blood was blue.

She sat up and looked at me in disgust.

"What the fuck was that for?" she asked, in a tone that sounded more pissed off than afraid. I threw the bat to the floor and grabbed her by the shoulders.

"What are you? What are you doing here?" I asked. "What's going on?"

"Which question shall I answer first?" she asked. I punched her again, and this time she grabbed me and threw me across the room. I saw stars as I slammed into the wardrobes at the back of the room, splintering the wood with the force of the throw. I then crashed into the floor. *Ouch…fuck…*

I bit my lip hard to stop from crying out in pain, and I looked back up at her with the most menacing expression I could drag up. But her face had started to change, and a cold, tingling horror washed over me.

Her features fused together, Jenny's face dripping off her like melted wax, dripping off her arms, chest, legs. What was underneath was a blue, slimy skin with long, bony limbs. It grew to over six foot within seconds. It was bald, with pale eyes, a long snout. Sharp teeth.

I literally almost shat myself.

"What's your fucking problem then?" it asked, sneering at me.

"What? What the fuck *are* you?" I asked, trying to not throw up again. I was still cowered in the corner of the room, I must have looked pathetic.

It just smiled at me, and I looked away, unable to stand the sight of something that hideous smiling. It crept towards me and knelt down so we were at eye level.

"Thanks for last night," it said. "It's been a while."

Oh God, I had sex with this thing, Oh God…Jesus Christ.

"Fuck you," I spat.

"You already did."

"Answer me. What's going on?"

It continued to inspect me, its eyes completely opaque. It then looked around the room, sniffing the air, licking its lips, pondering something.

My hand searched wildly for the pair of scissors that I had dropped a week or so ago down the side of the wardrobe, and I tried to maintain an even expression at the same time. As the creature returned its gaze to me, I stuck the scissors into its skinny chest in one fluid, terrifying motion.

It screamed in pain, and fell backwards onto the bed. It writhed around, trying to get back up, but its blue, gunky blood began to pour fast out of the wound. *All over my bed, great.*

It started to breathe slowly, deeply, its limbs twitching. It looked at me one last time.

"So...the proposal...I gave you the wrong answer?" it asked.

"Damn right you did," I replied. I took the scissors out of its chest and buried them into its neck. Its eyes bulged in surprise before it convulsed. I couldn't watch. I only turned back when it was still.

Damn right you gave the wrong answer.

To my shame and regret, there had never been a proposal.

CHAPTER SEVEN

Aria

Beth handed me a large mug of coffee. I was sat, dripping wet on their sofa. She sat next to Ash on another sofa, and they looked at me with friendly, expectant eyes.

I put the mug down on the coffee table; my hands were shaking too much. I shivered in my wet clothes. Beth saw this, and turned to Ash.

"Could you get her some of my clothes, please?" she said, and he got up and went down a small hallway and into another room.

I heard him shuffling around, opening and closing drawers. Then came a loud bang that made me jump, followed by Ash swearing. I saw Beth close her eyes in annoyance, exhale, and then open them again, her smile returning.

"I'm Beth, Beth Mulholland," she said. "The idiot over there is Ash Morgan. What's your name?"

Christ, I can't tell them I don't know! These people, no matter how nice they are, could still be working for those creatures. I can't trust anyone, not yet.

I looked around, trying to find something, anything that I could use as my name. A pile of books were in the corner, a picture of an orchestra, ornaments on a dresser table. *Fuck... think...anything... She's looking at you and the longer you wait the weirder it will be.*

I glanced at the name of the orchestra picture, and inwardly winced as I said the word out loud.

"Aria," I replied. My face flushed red.

"Aria? That's a nice name," she said. "What's your last name?"

For God's sake.

"Smith," I said.

"Aria Smith?" she repeated back to me, as though to make sure I was certain that that was indeed my name.

"Mmmhmm," I nodded. "Yep."

"Okay. Do you mind if I take a look at your face there, Aria?"

The first thing Beth did when we had got to the flat was give me a bag of peas to put over my swelling face. It was lying on the table next to the coffee, untouched. I couldn't even trust a bag of peas.

"Err, sure," I replied. She got up and met me so we were at eye level. She took my face in her hands, and turned it one way, then another. She then placed a cool, dry hand over the wound and swelling. I watched her close her eyes, and inhale, then exhale slowly. My face tingled, almost itched, and I was about to pull away when the pain and swelling was suddenly gone. She sat back on her heels, and I brought a hand to my face.

"There," she said. "All better."

"What…"

At that moment Ash came back with some clothes, and a towel. He handed them to me with a smile.

"I see Beth has taken care of you," he said. "She thinks she's Florence Nightingale."

"Fuck off," Beth replied. "The only time you're needed is when the kettle breaks."

Who are *these people?*

"Now," she said, turning back to me. I flinched when her eyes locked with mine. "You go shower, get changed, and then we can sort out how to help you, okay?"

31

I nodded blankly, and was led to the bathroom. I stood by the mirror, still dressed, for around fifteen minutes, looking at the stranger who was staring right back. My eyes were a hollow green, with large bags under them. My lips were dry, my hair was dark, messy, clumped up on my head. I was in desperate need of a wash.

Still in a daze, trying to process what exactly had happened to me, and why I didn't remember anything, I washed myself under the shower, trying to keep my desperate sobs of hopelessness quiet.

CHAPTER EIGHT

Freya

Weeks passed, and this... whatever this was inside me became stronger, more frightening. I woke in the night, horrified at the thoughts and dreams that took over my mind. At the same time, I felt like I was becoming part of something bigger, something more capable than I alone could ever be. It was thrilling.

My father told me I had become strange, disconnected, and he didn't like it. I told him I'd always been this way, and it had taken him this long to notice. Before he could strike me for being so rude, I left and went up to my bedroom, smiling.

A part of me was appalled that I could ever say such things to my loving father, but the rest of me simply rejoiced. I was becoming free, and my secret was helping me to do so.

However, every day it plagued me, I was afraid of what I was turning into. I was becoming almost inhumane; the thoughts, the feelings, it was indescribable... I knew evil was at the root of it, invading my body, my soul, but it was also my ticket out of this place and away from my guilt, pain, hatred and unfulfilled wishes. It seemed easier to feel nothing at all than to feel the pain I had felt before.

At first it was unbearable to watch my mother deteriorate, watching as my father tried to slow the blood from her opened wrists. He managed to, each time, and each time my mother woke up, shocked and alarmed that he had saved her. But after a while, I blocked it out, and eventually I didn't feel a thing for her. All I felt was power, and a hatred that I could not explain. This I managed to keep under control, until something happened that changed my life.

Even though I was enveloped in all these new feelings, I still enjoyed reading my books, and whenever I could, I still visited my usual sitting place, basking in the sunlight and absorbing every page and picture of each book that I had brought with me.

"Look, its her."

I heard the whisper, and looked up instinctively. There were the two girls, glaring at me as they walked past. My eyes quickly turned back to my book, and I tried to concentrate.

"Freya! Freya, you're so ugly!" one of them yelled.

"You almost look as ugly as your crazy mother!" shouted the other one. Bitch. My eyes burned, and bile rose to the back of my throat. I coughed and closed my book, setting it on the ground. My hands clutched the tree stump I was sitting on, digging into its mossy surface. My scalding eyes stayed fixed on the floor.

"Your mother is a whore, just like you!" the girl towards my left said. She was the taller of the two, and the eldest. I noticed that she was around my age, and my height.

"You are so disgusting; no wonder all the boys avoid the sight of you."

Closing my eyes, I fought down the urge to vomit.

They were saying the usual things they said, the kind of things they had always said, but this time I did not walk, or run, away. I was no longer a coward, no longer a pushover. I opened my eyes, and stood up, facing the two girls. Their eyes glistened challengingly, as if they wanted me to fight them. Not this time; I'd done that before, and it always ended with them laughing as I ran away, cradling my scratched face and my bruised limbs. My hair was usually blown away by the wind in clumps, as a good portion of it had been torn out. Not this time.

I walked slowly, and calmly, towards them, although my heart pounded and a voice in my head screamed for me to stop. They continued to look at me, delighted that they thought I was going to try and fight them. But the word fight implies that both parties have an equal chance, and I would not let them even touch me.

The taller one sniggered, and stepped towards me, ready to take her first swing. Her arm came round at the side of my head, but I grabbed it and threw it back. Her eyes widened and her mouth opened in confusion. I then reached out and took her neck in my hand, and gripped it hard. The girl was lifted from the ground, and with my heart thundering in my chest, I started to squeeze.

I felt the energy slipping away from this horrid girl, and I almost drank it up, wallowing in her horror. My fingernails dug deep into her pink flesh, and my arms easily batted away her feeble attacks. I kept squeezing, and heard her friend scream in terror. The girl's eyes bulged, almost popping out of her skull.

I was not aware of anything else around me; all I thought was that I wanted this girl dead, helpless, feeling if only for a second what I had been feeling since they started teasing me. The dark, evil thoughts inside took over. It was controlling my hand, but I let it. I could have stopped this, but the truth was that I absorbed every second, loving each sputtered breath and empty scream that the girl could muster. I only stopped squeezing when I felt a crack beneath my fingers, and the girl slumped underneath my palm. Her eyes grew dark, her limbs swung limply, and then came to a halt.

Only when I dropped the girl to the ground did I realise that I was crying, sobbing, hard. Trying not to be overcome by my emotions, I calmed myself quickly, and turned to finish what I had irreversibly started, but the other girl was gone. She had slipped away without my noticing.

This could be a problem.

CHAPTER NINE

Nick

I bombed down the road in my car, desperately trying to reach the café before Jenny left. Where had she been? What was happening to us?

I pulled up by the side of the café, and almost tripped out of my car. I ran inside, and watched the barista I had seen in my vision place a hand on a young girl's shoulder. *There she is. I'm not too late, I'm not too late.*

"Jenny!" I called, and her eyes followed the sound of my voice. Her gaze then fell on me and she sprung up and flew into my arms. I allowed myself to laugh, to be happy for a few seconds, before we had to sort out this mess. She hugged me so tightly, and cried into my chest. *This is my girl, this is my Jenny.*

"Where were you?" I asked her.

"I was there all night, I didn't know where to go, I'm sorry," she sobbed. "Everyone's dead Nick. Everyone's dead."

"I know sweetheart, I know," I replied. "Let's get you home, showered, and then we need to go to the police, tell them what happened."

She wiped her tears away and nodded.

"Yes, yes, we should," she said.

I led her out of the café, and placed her in the passenger seat of my car. I went round to my side and got in. We drove back to Laura's house in silence.

Jenny came back downstairs after her shower, and she had put on a baggy top and jeans. She looked so small.

"Here," I said, picking up her mug. "I made you some tea."

"Thank you," she replied, and took the mug. She then sat down next to me on the sofa.

"What happened there?" I asked. It was a vague question, but she knew what I meant. What craziness had happened at the facility? What had become of our friends? Why had those creatures tried to kill everyone, and burn the building? What did they want?

"I don't know," Jenny said, and sipped her tea. "But they were awful, horrible things. I've never seen anything like that in my life. They were hideous."

"They were," I said. I didn't know whether to tell her about the one who I had…who came back with me last night. It might have freaked her out too much. I didn't want to pile more on her than was needed now.

"When you're ready, we should go to the police station," I said. She paused.

"Do we have to go straight away?" she asked. "I'm so tired."

"But we are witnesses Jenny," I said. "We can tell them exactly what happened. It's already all over the local news."

"They won't believe us."

"They might. We can't just *not* say anything."

She was quiet again, and continued to sip her tea. I felt selfish then; she'd been through so much already. Maybe I was pushing her a bit too hard.

"I tell you what then, I'll go, I'll tell them everything, and perhaps they can arrange to come around here and take your statement? We don't even have to mention those creatures, we could say it was men, or wild animals, or…"

A fierce, blinding blow to my temple, followed by hot liquid burning my face, silenced me. I struggled to stay conscious, and turned to the creature. If it could make itself look like Jenny, who else could it turn into? They were shapeshifters. *This cannot be happening.*

"Sorry, sweetheart, we can't have you running to the police now, can we?" it said. The pain in my head muffled the shapeshifter's words, it was like cotton wool had been stuffed into my ears.

"What...the fuck..."

"What the fuck indeed," it said. I couldn't bear to open my eyes, the pain was too great, but I could hear that its voice had changed. It was no longer pretending to be Jenny.

"Look," the shifter continued. "Just stay out of the way. Leave her to us, and we will leave you alone. Let her go; she's as good as dead anyway."

"What do you want with her?"

"That's not for me to say," it replied.

They were there for Jenny then, they wanted her specifically. A memory then flashed into my mind's eye: Laura's face when I told her of my vision that the facility was going to be attacked by strange creatures. She didn't look surprised, almost as though she was expecting it. What did she know? She told me to evacuate the building, and meet her and Jenny at the house. Only they never turned up. I cursed Laura then for keeping such important information from us. Why didn't she trust me with this? I could have helped.

I finally managed to open my eyes, the hot tea still stinging them, and I looked over at the shifter, who was still sat on the sofa. It looked just like the other one, maybe a bit smaller. *I need to kill this thing, now.*

"So what do you say?" it asked. "Stay away, and we will leave you alone."

"I say you're fucking deluded if you think I'm going to let that happen," I said.

It laughed, throwing its head back. As it was so engrossed as to how hilarious it found itself, I eyed the prong on the mantelpiece that was used for the fire. I took it from its holder. The shifter stopped laughing, but didn't have enough time to move before I leapt forward and grabbed its neck. I stuck the prongs in, only a little bit, but enough for the shifter to feel it.

"Kill me, and another one will take my place," it laughed.

"I'm fine with that," I said, and plunged the prongs into its throat. It convulsed, struggled, gurgled, it was disgusting. I felt sweat creep down my forehead as I tried to keep the prongs inserted deep into its flesh. It was a relief when it was still. A few seconds later, the body turned to a strange, blue liquid mess on the sofa. The one upstairs must have done the same. *Gross; why do they have to bleed all over my furniture? I'll have nothing left!*

I threw the prong down and went to the kitchen for some ice. I found a bag of frozen peas and placed it gingerly onto my temple. I needed a plan, I needed to get information out of them, somehow. They would keep coming, keep distracting me, when I needed to find Jenny.

I glanced over at the set of kitchen knives, glistening in the morning sun. There was also a sturdy, wooden chair in the corner. I knew there were some ropes and locks in the basement downstairs. An idea formed, a disgusting, grotesque, wonderful idea. All I needed were some restraints. And some cigarettes.

I picked up my car keys and went to the front door. Just as I opened it, a familiar face appeared on the threshold.

"Hey baby," she said. "Where are you going?"

CHAPTER TEN

Aria

Half an hour later, I had showered, dressed myself in someone else's clothes, dried my tears, and stepped back out into the living room. Ash and Beth were waiting for me on the sofa.

I took a deep breath, thinking back to the willow tree, and sat down.

"Are you feeling any better?" she asked. I nodded; I couldn't think of anything else to say.

"I made you a sandwich," Ash said, and he produced a small plate of white bread, ham and cheese. It smelt heavenly, but I couldn't eat it, I didn't trust them enough to eat it.

"Thank you," I said, but I left it on the coffee table.

"Now, you don't have to tell us anything, if you don't want to," Ash continued. "But its not often we meet people like ourselves, and we knew you were one of the good ones, so – is there anything we can help with?"

Is there anything you can help with? Well…where do I start?

"What are you?" I asked him. It came out more rude than I had planned, but that was what I meant. What were these people? They weren't normal.

Ash threw back his head and laughed.

"We are normal people, we have jobs, we have families…not that we talk to them anymore…but, you know, we are normal, as I am sure you are too," Beth replied. "What exactly is your ability? I don't think I have seen anything like that before."

"I…I'm not sure," I replied. "I…It's just this energy…that's all I know."

"Okay. Aria, do you have anyone I can call? Someone who can come and pick you up?"

Tears pooled in my eyes again, and I looked down at my lap. I shook my head.

"Okay, that's no problem. Do you want to stay here the night? Get some sleep and we can look at this in the morning?" she said.

"I really should be going," I replied. For all I knew, these people would murder me in my sleep.

"We insist," Ash said. "And eat your sandwich before it goes warm. Get some sleep and we can talk tomorrow, okay?"

"But…why are you doing this? You don't know me," I replied. *Please just let me go, please.*

"We look after our own," Beth said. I looked at them again, and at that moment nothing sounded better than a good night's sleep.

"Thank you," I said to them. "That would be wonderful."

I woke up startled, uneasiness spreading over me like a blanket, as though I was late for something but I didn't know what it was.

My eyes opened sharply and the room came into painful focus, and I realised with a blind panic that I didn't recognise anything. But a few seconds later, the haze of sleep removed itself from my consciousness, and I knew, with a huge sigh of relief, where I was.

Yawning loudly, I stretched, and then winced as I remembered my body was still bruised and aching. I licked my dry, cracked lips, and tasted salt. I had been crying, and for a second my mind cast itself back to the dream I had woken up from. I was kissing somebody, I remembered my lips on their cheek, but it was so vague I couldn't remember who I was kissing, or if they were even male or female. Although I did remember a deep sense of sadness and loss wash over me. A bizarre, disembodied set of emotions for a person I did not know.

I glanced around, and took in the room that I had been too tired to scrutinize last night. There wasn't much to it as it was mostly unused, as Ash and Beth had their own rooms. There was a stack of unpacked boxes, various drawers and cupboards and a few ornaments dotted around. I noticed a large mirror in the corner, and I nervously went over to it.

I stood before the mirror, unsympathetic with its honesty, and flung my nightie over my head before my courage left me. I gazed in shock at the state of me. My frame was slim, my breasts small, yet my hips were wide, which looked a bit fun-house mirror against the rest of me. I traced myself with my hands, wanting to know everything about my own body. I grabbed about an inch of belly flab with my hands in dismay, and frowned at the cellulite on my bottom. My legs, however, were quite toned, as were my arms.

I was lost in the contours of my own body, so lost that I did not notice Ash walk into the room until it was too late, his pleasant smile turning into a grimace of embarrassment, his pale face turning pink. He immediately shut the door again as I scrambled to put my night-gown back on.

"I am so sorry," he said from behind the door. "I thought you would still be in bed. I, err… I brought you a cup of tea." My own face still aflame, I sat on the edge of the bed, tucked my legs underneath me, and smoothed down my mangled hair.

"You can come in now," I said to him, annoyed that my voice came out high and tight.

"Are you sure?"

"Yes, yes, come in."

Ash slowly turned the doorknob, and re-entered the room. His hair was wet and he was wearing black combat trousers and a plain white top.

He walked awkwardly to the bedside table, and placed a large mug of tea on the coaster, and stepped away again, back to the doorway. I eyed it suspiciously, but he saw me doing it, and sighed in exasperation.

"Aria, I don't know what you think we are up to, but I can promise you that its just a cup of tea. Drink it," he said.

My face flushed again, and I reached for the mug.

"Thank you," I muttered quietly.

In the brightness of day, and after a good night's sleep to clear my mind, I decided that so far they had not given me any reason to not trust them, so, as I had no other friends in the world it seemed, there wasn't much else I could do but let them help me.

"I'm really sorry again about bursting in," he repeated, "I should have knocked."

"Don't worry about it," I replied, giving him my best warm smile. "I guess it's not every day you have a strange woman in your flat wandering around naked."

He laughed at that, and the situation immediately became less awkward.

"I suppose that's true, unfortunately," he mused. "How are you anyway?"

"I'm good," I replied. "Thank you again for letting me stay."

"It's really not a problem," Ash said. "I…We just wanted to make sure you were safe. Do you want to talk about what happened to you? Is there anything I can do?"

I thought back to those creatures again, about how they ate that poor woman, how they nearly killed me. Why couldn't I remember who I was? Would telling Ash and Beth endanger them?

"I…I'm not sure if I should. I don't even really know myself," I replied, a bitter laugh escaping my lips.

"Okay, no worries…"

"I'm sorry, I just…I don't think it would help. I wouldn't know where to start," I tried to explain. It came out lame, which I knew it would, but saying everything out loud would make it more real, and I wasn't ready for that yet.

Suddenly, I had an idea.

"Do you have a town centre around here?" I asked.

He raised an eyebrow.

"Erm, no, we live in the wilderness, with fields and trees. I was actually up at five this morning milking cows…"

I threw a pillow at him, and he laughed.

"Sorry, yes, there is. I can drop you there if you like? What do you need?"

"Information," I replied. "And lots of it."

That afternoon, Ash pointed me to the nearest library before he went to work, and I made my way there. I was determined to find some clue about my past, something that would take me on the right path to getting my memory back. I walked inside the huge building, built over four floors, and asked if there was a section that covers local history and places of significance.

I decided to start with the latest newspapers, to see what had actually happened that night in the building. It wasn't long before I found several relevant articles.

"*Accidental fire kills dozens trapped inside*" "*Fire at a psychiatric clinic kills fifteen people*"

"*Fire started accidentally, experts say*" "*Families of the dead are seeking answers and compensation*"

The headlines whirred around in my head. The last thing that this was, was an accident. There was nothing about those creatures or the fact that half of the dead people had been eaten, only remains were left. The creatures must have burnt it down after I had left.

So it was a clinic for mental people, and I had no memory. No wonder nobody had come forward to claim me; I was a patient, I must have been.

Well, I'm not going back to a place like that again.

I spent four hours looking through old newspapers and books, trawling through them, scrutinizing every page until I finally came across an article about the hospital's opening in the 1970's.

A young doctor named Carl Murphy opened the building, along with a mixture of staff and other council officials. I didn't recognise any of the faces, but the article explained that it was opened in order to treat patients with severe mental problems, specialising in younger people. It was predicted to be a big success, and something that the city needed at the time.

There was nothing of much use, however, and although I got a little bit of background history, it just reinforced my suspicions that I was indeed a patient there. But what about the creatures?

There were more distraught parents threatening to sue and to claim compensation, but there was nothing that could tell me anything more as to how to find out who I was.

I tried looking up Dr Carl Murphy in telephone directories; he may have been able to tell me more, but he was not there.

I had another look at more online newspapers, and found nothing. It was as though I could disappear off the face of the earth and no one would bat an eyelid. After that I gave up, there was nothing to find. I was nowhere to be seen.

I knew then that I had to hide; they would lock me away again if I came forward.

No; this had to be my secret.

CHAPTER ELEVEN

Freya

I did not know how long I had been running for, or even where I was. I did know, however, that I would not be able to keep this up for much longer and eventually they would find me. My legs felt numb and yet ached so badly that I could hardly control where they were going. My lungs were bursting, and I felt light headed as I ran wildly through the trees. I was deep in the forest now, further than I had ever been before, I was sure of it. It was getting dark, and it became increasingly difficult to see where I was going. But I could not stop; they were behind me.

The other girl who had escaped had gone straight to her mother, who had in turn told everyone else and now they were all after me. I still could not take in what I had just done; for some reason it would not enter my head. I had taken a life, snapped that poor girl's neck, and all I felt was emptiness. The delight I felt after I had let the lifeless body slump to the floor soon disappeared, and I was left once again alone and forgotten.

My foot suddenly got caught under a group of tangled tree roots, and I fell clumsily to the ground. I heard loud, angry voices behind me shouting my name, and a female voice wailed in pure agony.

I shuddered at the sound, and tried to free my aching foot from the tangle of roots, but when I tried to move it all I felt was stabbing pain, and I feared I had broken it. I was stuck, useless and pitiful on the floor, waiting for them to do whatever they were going to do to me. The voices grew louder, and I closed my eyes, hoping they would not see me.

"Stand up, you evil creature," a gruff voice boomed. My eyes remained tightly closed, and I tried without success to free my throbbing foot. A large pair of arms grabbed my waist roughly and hoisted me up off the floor. My foot managed to untwist itself but there was a clearly audible crack. Pain shot through my whole body.

I screamed in agony and frustration, and tried to free myself from the thick pair of arms that had now lifted me up higher. I was being carried somewhere. I opened my eyes, and saw a mass of people equipped with torches, with children in tow, following this large, hairy man. I screamed and kicked with my good foot, but no one paid attention.

We entered a clearing, which was lit up with the light of so many torches. I was scared now; what were they going to do? Hang me? Burn me? It was not uncommon for criminals. I guess to them that was what I was; a sick criminal that had murdered their beloved child. The large man set me roughly on the ground, and I tried to land without putting too much weight on my foot, but I caught it on the dusty gravel as I stumbled and fell to the forest floor. I looked around, and saw people I knew and recognised from the village; people I saw at the market, people who used to greet me with a smile in the street. However no one had a smile for me now; there was just a mass of angry, crying faces.

Where was my power? My precious secret I had let take control of me? It was nowhere. Coward. This is your fault, I thought bitterly. You made me do it; you made me who I am now. I took a look at the large man who had carried me here, and saw he held something in his hands. It was a body, her body. I looked away, and he spat at the ground where I lay. I could not have ran away even *if my foot did not feel like it was about to fall off; everyone had circled around me, there was no way out.*

"Look at me!" he yelled. Tears ran down my face, and I turned my head slowly and looked him in the eyes. I tried to remain defiant but my quivering chin and shaking body gave away my fright. The large man neared me and set the cold, blue girl down next to me. It was only then that I noticed how beautiful she was. Long, golden hair, big eyes, neat slender fingers. She almost looked perfect, except the way her neck seemed a little misshapen. Her head did not sit right.

"Did you kill my daughter?" he asked. His eyes were like dark coals, and I knew with just the look he gave me that my answer did not matter. He was going to kill me anyway.

There was another wail from the crowd, and a dishevelled woman burst to the front row. She ran awkwardly to where the dead girl lay, and threw herself upon her, sobbing. It was her mother. I watched this scene without emotion, and at the same time I was horrified at my lack of guilt or feeling. I smiled at the crying woman, who was stroking the girl's long hair and whispering softly to her. The large man pulled the woman away and gestured for her to return to the crowd. To my terror a laugh escaped my lips, and then another. I giggled in delight at the misery of this poor woman; it made me stronger. I felt my power returning, it churned in my stomach, growing, feeding on her cries of sorrow, and I continued to laugh as I found that I was not alone anymore.

I abruptly stopped however, when a blow to my face sent me almost off the ground. My whole body turned around and I landed on the floor in a heap. I tasted blood almost immediately and felt that three of my teeth were now resting on my tongue. I spat them out.

"Did you kill my daughter?!" the large man boomed again, his body shaking with rage. Before waiting for an answer he pulled me

up from the floor by my shoulders and lifted me so we were eye to eye.

"Answer me," he whispered. His hands shook me violently, and I felt like I was going to vomit. When I did not answer he threw me to the ground again. Two other men were then upon me, they picked me up with ease even though I was screaming and biting, and roughly pushed me against a large tree. My hands were forced over my head, and a long length of rope was used to tie me tightly to the spot.

"Let me go! LET ME GO!" I screamed, trying to wriggle free, scared of what they were about to do. I felt so strange; I had never felt so panicked as I was at that moment, but at the same time I was calm, almost mocking their feeble attempts to be rid of me. No, that was not me; it was the power, or evil, inside me. It was not worried. Why? I was going to die.

In my struggle I did not notice that three hooded figures had closed in on me. They surrounded me, silent, and it was not until they started talking that I looked up to see what was happening. The three figures had their arms raised to me and I saw their grim faces stare blankly into my own terrified eyes. What was going on? Were they going to curse me? That's ridiculous; they would never do such a thing. Witchcraft is evil, and surely they would be fearful of such heresy? No, they would not risk it.

Still, as I told myself these things over and over, my heart pounded in fright, and I wriggled in vain to set myself free. I knew that if I was capable of taking an innocent life, these people were capable of doing whatever they wanted with me and they would be well within their rights. The figures started chanting, and I heard the sound of quiet drumming and rattling, although I could not hear what they were saying or where the drumming was coming from.

A part of me wanted to laugh at how ridiculous it all seemed, but the thought left my head as soon as it entered; I suddenly felt a pain inside me that I had never felt before. It was hot, searing, as though I was being ripped apart, or something was being sucked out of me. I screamed as I realised one of the hooded figures was actually making sucking motions with his mouth, as though he was sucking the life out of me. He held in his hand a stone, or some sort of crystal. My eyes blurred and my head felt fuzzy, and all I could hear were those chanting voices. They deafened me.

In my pain and confusion, I saw two familiar faces looking out at me from the crowd. My parents, they had come to save me. I felt an intense feeling of relief as I realised that the pain would soon be over. But they did not move, they did not even cry. They stared, unblinking, into my eyes. I wanted to shout out to them, to plead for them to come and save me. But my voice caught in my throat. Pain surrounded me, and I could not even think; I just wanted it to stop.

The last thing I saw before I hit total blackness was my mother's face; dry, old looking, and as though she did not even know me.

CHAPTER TWELVE

Nick

Exhaling the cigarette smoke into its face, making it cough, I took another drag before stubbing it out on its arm. It screamed in pain.

"Now, lets try again," I whispered as it glared at me. "Why do you want Jenny?"

I had managed to drag it to the basement and tie it up. I locked the basement door and left it in there shrieking, whilst I went to get some cigarettes. In terms of restraints, the only place I could think of what the local adult shop, so I bought a few sets of handcuffs from there. The only ones they had were red and fluffy, but they would have to do.

I had then returned to the shapeshifter. It was still struggling on the floor, trying to untie itself. I brought the wooden chair down from the kitchen and bolted it to the floor with some screws and my screwdriver. I grabbed it by the hair – it was still wearing its disguise – and I fixed it into place with the ropes and cuffs. The red fluff catching its eye, it began to laugh. I secured the cuffs just that little bit too tight, and it sucked in its breath, wincing against the pain. *Yeah, you laugh it up, you bastard.*

It then began to panic when I tied one long piece of rope around its neck, and looped it around a beam on the ceiling. I then secured it to the stair banister, keeping it taught. The shifter wasn't going anywhere.

"You've done this before, you kinky bastard," it smiled.

"Scouts came in handy for something," I shrugged.

My cigarette was then lit, and the questions had begun.

Half an hour later, I was no wiser. The shifter looked horrific – blood trickling down its disgusting limbs, its face bulging from the punches I had administered, welts from the cigarette burns, but it kept silent, only opening its mouth to moan or scream. I repeated my question.

"Why do you want Jenny?"

I pulled the rope that held the shifter's neck, tightening around its throat. The shifter gurgled and spluttered, trying to catch its breath. Just before it passed out, I let go of the rope, and the shifter gasped and groaned. I took the kitchen knife and made a small incision into its stomach. It wasn't deep, just enough to draw blood. It screamed. I cut it again. *Jesus Christ, what have I become?*

"Kill me," it said. "I won't tell you anything."

"Why?" I asked. "Why won't you tell me."

"The boss," it smiled through its pain. "You think you can torture me? You have no idea…"

I paused. I could sit here for a week trying to get information out of this creature, and it wouldn't tell me anything. Whoever this boss was, they were far scarier than I was at this point.

Frustrated, I stood up and threw the knife to the floor. It clattered for a second, and then it was still. Pacing the basement, I had to think about my next move. *What the hell am I going to do? I can't intimidate these things; they would rather die first.*

I turned to it once again. "Could you at least tell me if she is safe? Do you know where she is?"

"We are in the process of locating her," it replied.

"So you don't know where she is?"

It was silent.

"What happened to Laura?"

It smiled again, it was disgusting.

"We ate her."

No. I closed my eyes in shock. *Stay focused, come on, don't let this thing know that it just ripped your heart out.*

Just for that comment, just for the fact that it enjoyed telling me that piece of information, for the harrowing images it conjured up, I took the shifter's hand and cut off its middle finger. It screamed again, and slumped slightly as more blood poured from the wound.

I loved Laura like a mother, she was Jenny's mother, she was my family…and for her to die in such a way…I couldn't bear to think about it.

The shifter started to drift in and out of consciousness.

"Oh no you don't," I seethed. "You're not passing out on me you fucking pussy. Come on." I shook the shifter awake, and it groaned, opening its eyes.

"Kill me," it repeated. It's skin had gone a deathly grey rather than its usual blue. It was dying anyway. I pulled the rope tight, forcing the shifter out of the chair a little, and I looked away as it died. When it was still, it became what they all became, a big pile of nothing.

It was only then that I could acknowledge the hate that I felt for myself now. This shifter was evil, it needed to be put down, but was I any better? What did I do? What I had to? Or what I wanted to? I had used this opportunity to get all my frustrations out, to make someone else feel the pain that I was feeling. But it wasn't an excuse, this wasn't who I was. In mere days, I had become unrecognisable to the Nick I was before this all happened. But I couldn't stop, not now. Jenny needed me.

I decided to go to the police station, for a bit of normality of all things, and tell them what I knew. Hopefully their investigation would give me some answers too, something I could use to find Jenny. But first stop, the facility.

CHAPTER THIRTEEN

Aria

I was dreaming that I was in a park. The willow tree was there, and creatures were chasing me. I could smell the rain, the energy of the water washing over me. The tree was full of energy, full of life. I could feel everything. I could even feel the energy of the creatures behind me, they were black, empty, and they were going to kill me.

I woke up, sweat pooling around me. Confused, I looked around, and I sighed heavily as I realised where I was.

The past few days had been quiet. I had expected those creatures to come after me, to find me in Ash and Beth's flat, but no one had come. No one from my old life had appeared either, and I wasn't sure whether to be happy about that or not – if no one came for me, then I wouldn't have to go back to hospital.

I had learnt more about the two people I was currently living with though. Ash was nineteen, he worked in a nearby pub restaurant, and he was also an aspiring artist. He explained his ability as a "fire" behind his eyes, that he could manipulate the temperature of fluids. He had demonstrated by making me a cup of tea by heating the water with his fingers.

"It's about all I'm good for," he had shrugged, and it made me laugh.

Beth was a bit older at twenty-five, and she had trained as a nurse as the only thing she ever wanted to do with her life was to help people. She had such a kind nature; she even went out and bought me some new clothes. I had burst into confused, embarrassing tears when she presented them to me. *I don't deserve this kindness; I don't quite trust you, please stop doing nice things for me.*

To them, I was Aria Smith, a poor girl with abilities like them, who just needed a roof over her head for a while.

I had a hard time trusting these two people who had seemingly just taken me in out of the kindness of their hearts. Maybe it was that they had shown me the only kindness I could remember, and I didn't know how to take it. Either way, I kept my guard up.

I put on some clothes and made my way out into the kitchen. Ash was cooking something that smelled wonderful.

He turned to me. "Good morning, sleepy," he smiled. "Do you want some breakfast?"

God yes, yes I did. But did I trust what he was going to feed me?

I eyed what he had in the saucepan. There were sausages, eggs, bacon. *Oh God I have never smelt anything so heavenly in all my life!*

"I'll take that as a yes then," he said. He almost threw a mug at me across the table. "Here. Have some coffee."

"Thank you," I said. I looked around the kitchen. It was small and compact but there was a window that let in a few slivers of sunlight, and a few plant pots adorned the sill. The sun's energy fed the plant, the glistening, glittery tendrils of light beaming from its rays to the little stems and leaves. The transaction was beautiful.

I realised the flat was quiet. "Where's Beth?" I asked.

"She's at work," Ash replied. "Listen. I'm going out to get some bits after breakfast, do you want to come along with me?"

"Erm, well...I don't know..."

"Come on, its not like you have anything else going on," he laughed. It was meant to be a joke, I knew that, but it hit me like a blow to the gut.

I still hadn't told them anything about myself, and they accepted that for now, but Ash didn't realise exactly how much I didn't have going on, that he was more than right – I had no job, no friends, no family, but at the same time I had been running for my life for as long as I could remember, and my memory itself only stretched a few days.

He saw it in my expression, and his immediately fell.

"Christ, Aria, I'm sorry, I didn't mean…Okay, I'm a twat sometimes I know, but I didn't mean it that way."

"I know, don't worry, its me…I'm just…I don't know…"

Ash put down the frying pan and spatula and held out his arms. I shrunk away in panic. *Oh shit! This is it! He's going to kill me!*

But all that happened was that his arms enveloped me, and he pulled me into his chest, and held me tight. I let myself relax against him. After a few seconds, he let me go, and patted me forcefully on the back. I coughed.

"Now," he said, spooning the food onto a plate. "Eat up, and drink up. I promise its not poisoned, if that's what you're worried about."

I laughed half-heartedly.

"Oh gosh, no! Ha ha! No!" I replied. He raised his eyebrow at me and I stopped laughing, cleared my throat.

We ate in silence, every so often he stole confused glances at my flushed face.

"You just said 'gosh,'" Ash snorted into his food.

You idiot Aria.

58

I held some of Ash's shopping bags in my hands, glad to be of help. We had spent an hour at the supermarket, and now we were browsing a few of the market stalls before heading back home. It was a nice morning, the sun shone and people were milling about, mainly in good moods. I noticed that I could read faint auras emanating from people, their moods. Not much but it was there.

"I just want to stop here for a sec," Ash said, gesturing to a book stand. There were dozens of tattered volumes in rows, packed together in their respective genres.

"You like reading?" I asked.

"Who doesn't like reading?" he smiled. "You know how to read, right?"

"Of course I know how to read!" I said indignantly. "You flirt."

"You wish!" he replied with a smirk.

It was hard to not like this guy. I had tried to not trust him, to be wary, but I was instantly relaxed in his company, and despite the fact that strange, flesh eating creatures were after me, I felt safe in their flat. Especially with Beth there too; she was like an older sister. I was losing all the ways I tried to remind myself that these people were strangers.

"How did you and Beth meet?" I asked.

"Oh, years ago," Ash replied with a wave of his hand. "She... she helped me I guess."

"In what way?"

I saw a change in him then. There, behind the happy, sarcastic shell was someone with a dark past.

"Let's just say she was my only friend," he replied. "If it wasn't for her...well...I don't want to think about it."

"Sorry..."

"I guess we all have secrets, don't we Aria?" His tone was knowing rather than accusing.

"Yeah," I replied. "I guess we do."

I barely had time to register what had happened when someone struck me from behind. I felt pain in my head immediately, and I dropped the shopping bags. Ash turned in shock, and caught me before I fell. All I saw was a blur as someone in a dark coat flew past me. He was normal looking enough – brown hair, brown eyes, average build – but that *look* he gave me, that sickly smirk. He blinked, and for a second, his brown eyes turned pale. *The creatures.*

"Hey! You twat! What the fuck do you think you're doing?!" Ash yelled after him. I leant heavily against him as pain obscured my vision. I felt his heartbeat quicken. The creature ran off, carrying one of the shopping bags. *Why? For authenticity? Unless he needs to re-stock his fridge.*

"Ash…"

"That fucking nobhead just mugged us! I can't believe we've just been mugged!" he shouted. People had started to stare at us.

"Ash…"

"Shit, Aria, are you okay?" he then said, his attention on me. My head spun. I felt sick.

"I want to go home," I said.

"No worries, let's get you back," Ash replied. "We'll get you fixed up. Beth can take a look when she gets back. Fucking *arsehole!* I can't actually believe that just happened!"

He led me back to his car, and helped me in. The shock and terror, plus the pain in my head, had made me dizzy. It was only later that I realised what I had said. *Home.* I wanted to go *home.* And home was exactly where I felt at Ash and Beth's.

But a dread washed over me that morning and it never quite left; they were watching me, closing in.

And they wanted me to know it.

CHAPTER FOURTEEN

Nick

I stared in disbelief at the sight before me. On the way here I had geared myself up for charred remains of the building, for police tape everywhere, possibly a few officers. I had expected debris, tables, chairs, computers. The place had been ransacked and then torched, for God's sake, how can there be nothing left? There was nothing here, at all, just an empty field on top of a hill. You would never have known that a large psychiatric clinic had been here only a few days ago. Someone had this cleaned up quickly, and I could understand why.

Jenny, Laura and I, along with a number of others, worked at the Carl Murphy Psychiatric Centre, Carl Murphy not only being the founder, but a friend and respected work colleague. Even after he retired around a year ago, he still visited to make sure Laura, who became the new director, was getting on well.

But we weren't what the media thought we were. We specialised in 'ability management,' and counselling of issues that arose because of them. People of all ages and walks of life came to the facility, all with unique gifts, all wanting help, advice, and it was our job to tell them they weren't alone, and we could help them fulfil and take control of their abilities.

I knew about the facility because I was once a client there. My visions started when I was five, I didn't understand them, neither did my parents, and after losing Mark, my brother, they didn't want to lose me too. I grew up coming here. I met Jenny here.

When I left school, this was where I wanted to be, to work and help others like me.

And now look at it, it was as though it had never been there at all.

I took one last look at what had become of my livelihood, before I made my way to the police station.

I parked the car and entered the police station, trying to shake the accompanying nervousness I felt by merely being here; as though I was turning myself in for something.

It wasn't busy, but I made sure to avoid eye contact with all the other people sat waiting in the reception area. I wasn't really sure why.

I was told to take a seat, and a few minutes later a young police officer called me over. She smiled warmly, which made me feel a bit better.

"How can I help?" she asked. Her features were rather small, but her eyes were a light brown, large, inviting me to spill everything to her.

"Well," I began. *Where do I start?* "I'm not sure really. I used to work at the psychiatric centre that burnt down. I…I wanted to make a statement."

Her eyes widened. "You're a witness?"

"Yes."

"Okay, no problem. Come with me, I'll book us a private room."

When I finally got out of that room around half an hour later, I was even more angry and confused. *And scared, terrified.*

I lit a cigarette and smoked it pensively beside my car. I needed a drink.

Withholding all mention of shapeshifters, I told her that the fire was started by people who had broken in, murdered everyone who was there, and then burnt the place to the ground. She raised an eyebrow at me, which I found slightly irritating. I should have known who she really was in that moment, but once again hindsight remains both arrogant and useless.

She told me that the fire was accidental, an electrical fire, and the 'unfortunate casualties' died from smoke inhalation. I was struck by her tone, the way she said it as though it was rehearsed, the glint in her eye. I realised then that it was a cover up, a conspiracy. *How many shifters had taken over around here? Could I be sure she was one, or was I being paranoid?*

I asked how she knew all this; it would take weeks, perhaps months of investigation to determine that, plus the bodies that must have been recovered – last time I checked, smoke inhalation doesn't cause your guts to rip open and devour themselves.

She said this is what has already been stated in the press releases.

I told her that all this evidence could have been retrieved from the building, it was arson, and it was murder.

"What building?" was all that she said. I left quickly after that.

I would have to figure this out on my own.

I got home with another pack of cigarettes and a bottle of Jim Beam. I never used to drink much, only at social occasions really, but there were a lot of sorrows to drown, and what the hell? I had nothing left to lose.

I sucked greedily on the cigarette, and inhaled deeply. I then took a swig from the bottle, and winced at the taste and the sensation of it burning my throat. *Gross.*

After I stubbed out the cigarette, I looked through the phone book to find Carl's name. Perhaps he could tell me what was going on, if he knew who these creatures were, if he had ever seen them before.

He wasn't in there. I tried Laura's address book, and surprisingly it wasn't in there either. I tried googling him – there were no contact details available. I had no way of getting in touch. It would have to wait.

I dropped the bottle down heavily onto the coffee table as my vision hit me. I was sat on my sofa, as I already was, but someone was next to me. *Mark.*

He looked sad. He was looking at me, did he know what was happening? Was this all in my imagination? Because I wanted to talk to him so *badly*? He was a man now, when the last time I saw him in real life was when I was five years old, and I didn't really remember that.

"Hey," I said. "Hope you're doing better than I am mate."

The corners of his mouth twitched, it was almost a smile. Then my vision ended.

Since Mark had disappeared twenty years ago, this was all I ever saw of him now, I don't even know if it's real. He just disappeared when he was ten, and our family never really got over it. My parents assume now that he is dead. But me…I hold out hope that he is there. And sometimes, I feel him in the room, I feel him next to me, and its as though we are kids again. But it lasts a few seconds, and then that's it; once again I am on my own.

Jenny helped me through a lot of this, back in the days when it really got to me. As a teenager, when my visions were really bad and I would end up bedridden for days, she would be there, to take my mind off it, to entertain me, to bring me soup and magazines. I always thought she was cool. And her abilities… they were something else. They were amazing, beautiful, her connection to nature…it suited her personality. She would always bring out the abilities in others too; heighten their natural powers. *Why hasn't she got in touch?* She was either dead, or they have her.

The thought made me feel sick, but it made sense. She wouldn't do this to me; she wouldn't leave me wondering about whether she was alive or dead, she knew I loved her more than anything in this world. I had to find her.

I had to kidnap one of these shifters and step up my game. They would talk, eventually. I would make them.

CHAPTER FIFTEEN

Aria

I awoke once again to the sounds of screaming, dead eyes, jaws that snapped and barked and large creatures that lunged for me. I couldn't get out, I couldn't find help, or breathe, or even *see*. *Where am I? What is this holding me down?*

When the haze of nightmare cleared, I realised that I was wrapped up inside the covers, cocooned, with my head underneath the pillow. I couldn't see a thing, and with what might have been a hilarious struggle if anyone had happened to see me, I freed my arms and shuffled and twisted out of the covers. I was covered in sweat once again. *Nice.*

I fought the urge to cry out to my flatmates, I was weird enough without these incidents happening. And they had done so much for me already.

Ash and Beth had welcomed me into their home and into their lives without hesitation. They had fed me, clothed me, put a roof over my head, even when I didn't trust them, and they knew that. But these people had saved me, and I owed them everything. They were the only people in my life. The only people I could call friends. Even though a few weeks had now gone by, no one from my old life had come forward to claim me, and why would they?

Apart from the dreams, I had decided to leave my old life behind, and start afresh.

After the incident in town, I had seen no more of the creatures. Nevertheless I remained wary; they were always there, in the back of my mind, and I knew at some point, they would come for me.

I decided to have a shower, if nothing else than to clear my head of the dreams.

Lathering some shampoo up in my hair, I let the smell enter my nostrils. It smelt of apples. Reaching for my razor at the side of the bath, I started to shave my legs. I noticed the water get a little hotter, and so I turned down the dial a little.

I had been doing exercises to try and remember who I was, something I had googled at the library. After the initial panic of having no memory had left me, I decided to go about it as something I needed to find again, like a type of mission. Even if it never came, even if I was like this because I was a patient with possible brain damage, at least I would try.

The shower water became increasingly hotter, and I turned the dial down again until it was pointing to the cold-water symbol, only it wasn't cold. I rinsed my hair, wondering when I should go and get it cut; it was looking a little shabby.

Suddenly, an immense pain washed over me. It felt like someone had poured the contents of a boiled kettle onto my skin, and I screamed in shock and pain. I cracked my back on the side of the bathtub as I tried to jump out of the way of the burning water.

I crawled out of the bathtub, letting a cry ring out around the otherwise quiet flat, and I tried to catch my breath, gritting my teeth in pain. Tears stung my eyes.

I sat up, and saw that the skin on my legs had almost sizzled, and I felt that the skin on my back must look similar. Grabbing a towel from the rack, I was just able to cover myself when Beth barged in, her eyes wild.

"What?! What?!" she cried, almost stumbling over her own feet. She was in nothing but a dressing gown tied at the waist, I must have woken her from her sleep. I tried to stand up but my legs wouldn't move.

"The water was too hot," I said. "I...I burned myself...sorry..."

I gestured to my legs, and Beth stared at them in horror. The pain was too much.

"Okay, shush honey don't worry," she said, and I tried to hold together my shaking body.

"Oh, God..." I whimpered. It was getting worse. I thought I could smell my own burnt skin.

Thankfully, Beth worked quickly. I felt her hands on my skin, the familiar tingle, and I bit down on my lip against the agony of holding still. Then, the pain was gone.

I began to sob with relief, and I hugged her as hard as my shaking arms would allow. My body was still in shock from the pain, but at least it was over. At least I didn't have to bear it anymore.

"Thank you," I whispered. She hugged me back. "Thank you so much."

She then sat me down on the chair in the bathroom, and went to feel the water that was still running from the shower. I shouted for her to stop, but then saw that she held her hand there, not flinching or pulling away in pain.

"Its fine now," she said as she turned the shower off. "But our landlord is *so* going to hear about this."

Ash then scrambled out of his room. He didn't come into the bathroom, but he stood just behind the door and shouted.

"Are you guys okay in there? What happened?" he asked, his voice high with panic.

"The fucking shower's broke," Beth replied. "It burned Aria."

"*What?* Jesus Christ! I'm so sorry Aria," he said.

"It's fine, Beth sorted me out, really, don't worry." I felt a bit

68

silly then, and wrapped the towel more tightly around myself. *I'm making too much of a fuss.*

"It's not fine," Beth said, and she helped me up. She held the towel around me as she assisted me to the spare bedroom, although I was completely fine physically, I still felt sick from the pain. Ash was just outside the door. He looked shocked.

"I'm fine, really," I said to him.

"I'm sorry," Ash repeated, quieter this time. Beth looked over her shoulder at him, but I couldn't see her expression. She shut the door rather forcefully and then laid me down on the bed.

"You should get an hour's rest, I think," she said. "I'll get Ash to phone the landlord about the shower."

"I'm really sorry for causing all this fuss," I replied. "I didn't mean to."

"Shh, don't worry. You just get some rest now. I'll be in if you want some food later or something."

I yawned loudly, not realising how exhausted the shock and adrenaline rush had made me. I then felt a wave of nausea hit me, and I had to close my eyes to fight it. *For God's sake don't be sick on their carpet, please Aria; you've embarrassed yourself enough.*

"Thank you," I said.

Beth just winked at me and then closed the door. I was asleep in seconds.

Later that evening, I was sitting at the windowsill of my bedroom.

I thought back to what Beth had done for me, and what she had done the first day I had met her. She truly had a gift, and I was glad that she could use it every day to help people. These kinds of gifts should be cherished, and what excited me most was that I felt that I had dealt with this before, as though these kinds of occurrences were not totally alien to me.

Watching the trees sway and the sun duck behind clouds, I felt something stir inside me. My hands started tingling, and I looked down to see green sparks of energy coming from inside, and out through my finger tips. I suddenly wanted, so badly, to be outside.

I looked back down at the people wandering about in a new light. It was the same feeling that I had that day in town, only stronger. I could see their auras, I sensed their moods, their emotions; they were plain for everyone to see. There were bright blues and greens, attached to people laughing happily together and enjoying the sunshine. Colours that I had never noticed before now dazzled in front of me. There were shades of green, brown, blue, purple; they were all over these people.

There was a couple holding hands, walking down the road with eyes only for each other, their auras the exact same deep purple. They were in love.

I saw the bright green flecks of jealousy in a young girl whose friend had just bought herself a new handbag. There was a boy of around eight or nine whose black and red aura showed me he was grieving. He wiped his eyes with his sleeve as he held tightly onto a dog's chew toy. His mother was quietly trying to console him.

I then noticed a dark, grey aura surrounding a middle-aged man walking down the street. His movements were slow and he drew deep, laboured breaths. His clothes were smart, professional, and he carried a laptop bag over his shoulder. He was carrying on with his daily life, ignoring what was churning inside. I couldn't help but wonder if he had even told anybody at work, or perhaps his parents, or a wife or girlfriend, that he only had a few months to live. The grey surrounding him was an illness of some kind. I then noticed the dirty, yellow specks in the grey, dancing around like glitter. They had settled on his chest, and he stopped to cough momentarily, leaning on a wall. The yellow specks shuddered as this happened, and when the fit of coughing ceased, they settled once again on his chest. *Lung cancer.*

As soon as it had appeared, I felt the energy leave me, and that sunny street of people became anonymous again, where I didn't know anybody, and I couldn't read a thing they were feeling.

I watched the man, who now almost looked like everybody else. He walked slowly, painfully away. I pressed my hand against the cold glass, as though that action alone could somehow save him, and wished him well, if only for a short time.

CHAPTER SIXTEEN

Nick

The next shapeshifter that revealed itself to me didn't even bother trying to pretend. Word had obviously got back to the rest of them, that there was no need to try and trick me anymore, that we all knew the game plan. What they didn't know was mine. *Just keep sending them to me, and I'll bleed the information out of them.*

They thought they were distracting me whilst they did whatever they were doing with Jenny. It wasn't distracting, it was therapeutic, cathartic even. I itched to inflict some pain, to get some answers.

The disgusting creature, still disguised as Jenny, just walked through the door, flung it open with such a force that I thought the door would come off its hinges, and grabbed me. I didn't have much time to do anything else but let it pick me up and throw me against the wall, smashing a few trinkets.

I hit the floor with a dull thud, smacking my knee against the wooden floor, but I sat up with a smile on my face.

"I was beginning to think you guys had forgotten me," I said.

The shifter grimaced at me darkly. It shed Jenny's features within seconds to reveal the true creature beneath.

"Come to distract me some more?" I asked.

It crouched on the floor, its sharp elbows and knees jutting out from under its thin skin.

"No," it breathed. "New orders are to kill you."

"Had enough of me already then?"

"Something like that."

"Well come on then," I said. "I'm right here."

I crouched down to meet the creature at eye level, my face inches from its own.

"Kill me."

It grabbed my arms and bit down hard into my left shoulder. I felt it hit bone. It tore away a large chunk of flesh and I fought nausea as I watched it eat it. My blood dripped from its mouth and onto the floor, and I reeled from the pain, clutching the wound. *Don't pass out, not until after this is over.*

It lunged for me again, but I caught it this time and watched in disgust as it snapped its jaws at me. Its breath reeked of rotting meat. I forced it back and took out the knife I had been keeping in a holder on my belt, for an occasion such as this. Despite it being just a normal kitchen knife, it was sharp, and big enough to be a threat to this thing crawling around in front of me.

"You taste awful," it said. "Like ash."

"I'm an acquired taste," I replied, my other hand still holding the wound, trying to stem the flow. "I think you should have another try."

It didn't need me to ask twice. It leapt from its crouching position, almost hitting the high ceiling, and stretched out its wiry arms for me. My heart pounded sharply, pushing out more blood from my wound, but I had to trap this creature before I became too weak. I drew back the knife with a shaking hand, and plunged it into the shifter's shoulder. I gasped with the effort. It fell to the floor, and I took out another knife and stuck it in the other shoulder, pinning it down. I almost fell over when I then reached for a length of rope, my own blood dripping onto it, but I had to secure this bastard if I had any chance of keeping it there.

I tied its legs together, and I tied its neck to a pair of hooks that

I had installed on the floor, so it was stuck, impaled. That was how I needed it.

I went to dress my wound before continuing, afraid that I would lose consciousness before my interrogation was complete.

After my incident at the police station, a dread and sense of urgency had washed over me – who knew how many of them were out there – perhaps hundreds. I couldn't trust anybody. I had to find Jenny, it plagued every step I took. I couldn't eat properly, I smoked and drank too much, I barely slept.

So I had kitted out Laura's house with traps and restraints, more weapons, a first aid kit. I had then got drunk and waited, smoking God knows how many cigarettes in the process. I was ready, waiting for one of them to return.

I used the gauze and cotton from the first aid kit to dress my shoulder, put in place with some tape, and not bothering to put another top on, I calmly faced the shifter.

It had stopped struggling, and was looking at me with what I hoped was fear. It looked like fear. Tensing my shoulders, I punched it in the face, just to see what it would do. But it remained still, letting me rain blow after blow over it. Only when its jaw snapped, dislocated and hung loosely from its face, did it start squirming, yelping like a dog. I twisted the knives in deeper, and it screamed.

After an hour, it was dead, beaten to a pulp, and I ended its life with a swift knife to the chest, and let it puddle on the floor.

I lit a cigarette and smiled, trying to ignore the bile rising from my stomach, my bleeding knuckles, my aching guilt, because it was the first one to talk. It was the first one to give me any kind of information about what was going on. It was the first to give me a name, two even.

Ash. And Beth.

CHAPTER SEVENTEEN

Aria

The following night, Ash arrived home at around 11:30pm after his shift at the pub. Beth would be at work until the morning, and I had been sat on the sofa with the TV on, but once again trying to do my memory exercises. I had a green ball of energy in the palm of my left hand, and I exchanged it to my right hand, then back again. *What does all this mean? What is the purpose of this energy? Is it truly mine?*

Ash greeted me as he entered, and then turned and locked the door.

"So, fancy a drink?" Ash asked.

"Do we have any whiskey?" I asked. If Ash was in the mood for a drink, then so was I. He went to the kitchen to check.

"Yep!" he said loudly, and then brought in the bottle and two glasses.

"Thanks," I said as he poured me some. After he poured his own we clinked glasses and then drank. He nearly gulped down the whole thing in one go, whereas I opted to be more lady-like and took small sips.

We sat back together on the sofa and talked. Ash liked talking about the future; about where he would like to be in the next five years, and what he would like to be doing. It was inspiring to listen to him; it made me feel anything was possible.

"I've been looking on the internet for University courses around here," he said excitedly.

"Oh yeah? What did you find?" I asked, taking another sip of my drink. It tasted awful but it warmed my stomach.

"Well, I was looking at art courses, and it costs three thousand a year for tuition fees."

"Wow, that's a lot."

"Yeah, I know, but you can get a loan to cover it, and grants for living costs. I think if I keep working part time during the course I'll be able to enrol possibly next year."

"Sounds like a plan," I said cheerfully.

I thought back to when Ash had shown me some of his drawings and sketches; they were always so beautiful. Some were of objects like ornaments or the view outside a window, but he said those were more of his 'boring' drawings, and what he really liked to draw was figures captured in some sort of powerful emotion, like a couple kissing passionately, their arms around each other, dead to the world, or the fear in the face of a young soldier running forward into battle, or even the happiness shown in a sketch he entitled "Companionship," of an old couple sitting together, laughing at a private joke, their faces warm and their eyes shining. He told me he had seen them once sat on a bench together when he went for a walk in the park, and he had to draw them, to savour that moment of pure happiness.

He also once showed me a sketch entitled "Loss", in which I could almost feel the pain of the boy who had slashed his wrists, and was knelt over a photograph of a girl, his face riddled with torment and grief. It had brought tears to my eyes. Ash could really portray the hurt, anger, lust or whatever he wanted in these drawings. I thought they were fantastic.

"Yeah, that's my plan," he said. He poured himself some more whiskey, and then offered the bottle to me. I took it and refilled my glass. "So what's your plan, then?" he asked.

"Well," I said, thinking. "I'm not sure. My life is pretty okay at the minute; can't complain."

"Surely there must be something you want to do with your life? What are you interested in?"

I honestly didn't know; it was a hard question to answer. *What I would really like is my memory back.*

"I suppose I wouldn't mind travelling someday, after I've saved enough money," I finally replied. "I'd like to go to Egypt…"

"Me too! I'd love to go there," Ash smiled.

"Well that's settled then, we shall go to Egypt together!" I said triumphantly, and we clinked glasses again to seal the deal. We both drank to that and I then put down my empty glass, and then swiftly reached for the bottle again.

Around half an hour later my head began to swim. I was lying on the sofa, and a drunken Ash was sprawled on the chair next to me. He was going on about something or other, gesturing so hard with his arms that he nearly spilt his drink all over himself.

I left him to his ramblings, and sat back into the sofa pillows. I thought about what he had said earlier; did I really not have any plans for the future? I had no idea. Ash was good at something; he had a gift with drawing that could be put to good use in many different career paths, but I didn't know how to do anything. Well, more precisely, I wasn't particularly good at anything; I was average. Although, I would need to start looking for a job soon; I couldn't expect them to keep me forever.

"Hey, have you done any more drawings recently?" I asked, trying to focus on Ash's face. Ash looked at me and took another sip of whiskey.

"Erm…a few think," he replied, closing his eyes.

"Would it be alright if I had a look?" I asked before trying in vain to stand up from the sofa, leaning on the wall for support.

My mouth felt dry and my head was still swimming. I made my way clumsily to Ash's room after seeing that he could hardly sit up, never mind stand.

"Hang…hang on a minute!" I heard Ash drawl back in the living room.

"It's okay, I'll get them!" I shouted back. I switched the light on and stood still for a few seconds, breathing heavily, wondering where he kept his drawings. I could hear him shuffling around in the living room, banging into things, and I wished he would sit back down before he hurt himself.

I looked on his shelves that were full of papers and several weird looking objects that I couldn't quite focus on. I thought I saw a rather unnerving dragon ornament on the second shelf; its mouth was wide and twisted into a snarl. I looked away quickly and eventually found his scrapbook. I rushed back to the living room, grazing my arm on the wall as I banged into it and slumped back down onto the sofa.

"Found them!" I announced, opening the first page. Ash had his eyes closed, and he whispered something to me, something I couldn't make out.

"What?" I asked, turning to him. His eyes were still closed and he was rubbing his temples with his hand.

"Can you…put them back?" he whispered to me, putting a hand firmly in the middle of the scrapbook. But I had already opened it. My eyes managed to focus, and I saw a beautiful drawing of a girl, stood alone in the rain. Her eyes were bright but she looked incredibly sad.

"Hang on," Ash said more sternly next to me. "Those ones… aren't finished."

"They look pretty finished to me," I said, lifting his hand away and turning the page. There was another picture of a girl, possibly the same one, only this time she was in the shower…I turned the page quickly. There she was again; her eyes closed, her mouth smiling. She was on a bed, naked, the covers hanging loosely just above her waist. *He's drawn her breasts.*

I closed the book, my face turning red. No wonder he didn't want me to see them.

"Sorry, I didn't mean to…" I said, putting the book down.

My heart pounded painfully in my chest, and part of me wanted to run away and never come back. I should have kept my hands to myself and not on sifting through other people's belongings. "Is she anyone we know?" I asked after a pause. I didn't expect him to tell me, but I would have said anything at that point to extinguish the awkward silence that surrounded us. I wished I hadn't been so nosy. Ash looked away from me and finished his drink.

"You know who it is…please don't make me say it."

I recognised the girl, but if I spoke these words out loud, it would make this real. Did I want this to be real? But what if I was wrong? What if they weren't of me at all?

"They can't be drawings of…well, of me," I said, laughing as the words came out, trying to lighten the oppressive atmosphere. I instantly regretted this when I saw the look on his face.

It said it all.

"I'm sorry," he said. "I shouldn't have drawn them. You're my friend, and I want to be yours, but…"

"It's okay," I interrupted. I didn't want him saying anything to me that would further embarrass us both in the morning. "It's fine really. Here…" I handed him the scrapbook. "I shouldn't have snooped, I'm sorry."

He looked at me with a fierceness that I had never seen before, and I couldn't help but look back. He leaned in closer to me, and I knew what was about to happen.

I didn't have much time to think about whether I wanted this, before he kissed me. It was a hard, drunken kiss; it didn't feel right. *Aria, you need to stop this, stop this now. You don't want this, don't hurt him.*

But suddenly his hands were running through my hair, over my face, down my back. I was lost in the fact that I couldn't remember anyone ever kissing me before, and it was wonderful. His mouth was so warm.

But something was nagging at the back of my mind. Someone else used to kiss me like this, someone else…who? And where were they? They couldn't be that bothered about me.

I was using Ash to try and forget the shithole that was my life. I kissed him harder, heard him sigh.

There was a strange sound, like a loud *pop*, and then, my eyes still closed, I was hit with small, sharp shards. They sliced into my arms, my face, and Ash and I jumped away from each other in shock. *Oh God, the creatures are here!*

I looked around. It was glass. Where had it come from?

My whiskey was all over the floor, amongst bits of glass. My drink had exploded. *What?*

"Oh my God, I am so sorry, I didn't mean…I'm sorry."

He took my arms in his hands and turned them around. I saw that he too had small shards of glass sticking out of his arms, but he didn't seem to notice them.

"What…what just happened?" I asked. I began to pick out the glass. Blood trickled out of the tiny wounds. *Ouch.* Then I realised what he had just said to me.

"Why are you apologising?" I asked. Ash's face then turned from concern to shock and fear; he had said something he wasn't supposed to.

"I didn't mean to, I don't…I don't know what's going on. It just happened, I'm sorry. Are you okay?" He was trembling; I could see he was just as scared by the incident as I was.

"Ash? What's going on?" I pressed.

"I…I don't know. My abilities just recently, I can't seem to control them. They're becoming stronger, too much, sometimes, I'm so sorry Aria."

I thought back to a few nights ago…the shower, the pain I felt before Beth healed me, and I felt an anger rise in me that I had never felt before.

"Did you have anything to do with what happened in the shower? You know, when I was burned?"

He looked away from me then, and I knew the answer before he even said it.

"Yes," he finally replied.

"Jesus Christ, Ash!" I yelled, my calm completely gone. "Do you know how painful that was? If Beth wasn't there I don't know how it would have ended up. I could have been scarred, did you think about that?"

Ash then glared at me, the look in his eyes was like nothing I had ever seen before. I really thought at that point that he was going to hit me, or hit something, and I knew I had said the wrong thing. I stiffened in fright.

I almost jumped out of my skin when he moved, but all he did was reach down to the bottom of his shirt. He pulled the shirt over his head and turned around so I could see his back. He did it slowly. My eyes fell on something I almost wished that they hadn't.

A burn scar ran across his shoulder blade and down his back. It looked grainy and bobbled, as if someone had put a sheet of bubble wrap under his skin. I fought the urge to reach out and touch it, to test its surface. I was speechless.

He pulled down his shirt again and turned back towards me.

"When I was little my older sister accidentally spilt hot water from the kettle on me. It could have been a lot worse apparently. I don't really remember it happening, but I sometimes get edgy around hot things, as if my body remembers something my brain doesn't."

I blinked, a feeling of déjà vu sweeping over me for only a moment. I stared at him in disbelief.

"I'm sorry, I didn't know…how could I have not known this? I live with you!" I said.

"I hide it well," he replied. "Please believe that I would never intentionally hurt you."

"I know, I'm sorry," I said.

I pulled my chair closer to his and wrapped my arms around him. He hugged me back, and we stayed there for a while in silence. I owed him my life after all; there was nothing he could ever do that would change the fact that he saved me, and took me in.

"Why do you think your abilities have changed?" I asked him.

He pulled away from me.

"Okay, don't hate me," he replied.

"Promise?" "It depends on what you say," I said, raising an eyebrow.

"Okay, well I think it might be you," he replied. "Your energy. I don't know, I just feel stronger when I'm around you."

I wanted to be angry with him, I wanted to shout and tell him how dare he say such a thing, but I knew he was right. Whatever was inside me, it was powerful, and I didn't fully understand it.

Ash put his hands up to his face and exhaled heavily. He then ran his fingers through his hair.

"You know the drawing in the shower?" he asked. "Well I was

drawing it at the time you were burned. I didn't know what would happen, that the water would grow so hot like that. I was just thinking about you, that's all."

His voice had become a whisper as he hung his head, once again unable to look at me. I really didn't know what to say. I just stared at him, wondering how I hadn't realised he felt this way about me. Was I so ignorant to the people I cared about?

"I'm going to bed," he said.

"Yeah, me too."

We both left the living room and entered our bedrooms in silence.

CHAPTER EIGHTEEN

Nick

I was dreaming about her again, I knew that. But it was the tiniest respite I could allow myself from all the horror of the past few weeks. She had been missing for almost a month now, and as I felt her skin, felt her kissing me, lying next to me in my bed, I acknowledged it wasn't real, but I made love to her anyway.

I held her and made her scream, watching her face screw up the way it does when she orgasms, and I let myself come inside her.

When I woke up, all that met me was the emptiness of Jenny's room, and a sticky mess in between my legs. *I'm so pathetic.*

I had moved all my stuff from my flat to Laura's house, since I spent most of my time here. No one was occupying it anyway, and it would save me on rent payments. I had some savings that would keep me going for a few months.

I had rigged the place up for capturing shifters, and I had used it as a base for researching the two names I was given. Ash and Beth.

They weren't too hard to find, I found their address easily, their last names, where they both worked.

I had their contact details pinned up on the fridge, and I had parked up a few times and sat outside the building where their flat was located. *How do these people fit into what is happening?* I hadn't seen much except glimpses of them going to and coming from the building. I followed the girl, Beth, to the hospital where she worked, and I had followed Ash to the pub, but I couldn't see anything incriminating.

Had the shifter lied to me? Did it give me two random names that led me on a subsequent wild goose chase? Perhaps they had nothing to do with Jenny at all.

Today I was going to follow them one last time, and if they seemed ordinary, I would just leave them alone. Either that, or kidnap them for questioning, I hadn't decided yet.

I showered, wiping away the excess cum from my thighs, feeling ashamed that I should let things like this happen when she was still missing, possibly hurt, probably dead. How could I think about self gratification at a time like this? I loved Jenny more than anything, and to think that she was out there somewhere, in pain, wondering where I was, I just couldn't bear to think about it. Masturbation should be low on my list of things to do, and wet dreams? Was I thirteen? But I couldn't help it, I missed her physically as much as emotionally. Maybe it all meant the same thing.

After I was dressed, I put my boots on and my jacket, lit a cigarette and left the house. I had grown to find cigarettes comforting, I wasn't sure why, but perhaps at this point I could allow myself this small luxury.

I drove to the flat, and waited for something to happen. I had found which windows belonged to Ash's and Beth's flat, and I watched them closely.

After half an hour, nothing had happened, and my growling stomach had begun to distract me. I was about to leave to get some food, when I saw someone coming out the front door of the building. It was the boy, Ash, closely followed by the girl. There was another girl… *What? Another shifter! What is it doing there?*

It was disguised as Jenny again, but I knew that the real Jenny would not be living with such strangers, she would have come straight to me. Were these people then in danger of the shifters? Were they innocents that I had to protect?

They didn't seem disturbed or scared in any way, in fact they were laughing and talking as they all piled into a car. The car started, and I automatically started mine and began to follow them.

CHAPTER NINETEEN

Aria

There was a hand on my cheek; it was large, firm, and yet gentle. I couldn't see or hear, or sense anything around me save for this warm flesh cupping my face. I had no worries, no concerns, everything melted away. I remembered, in my dream, I remembered for a second who it was, what they meant to me, and it made me feel sick.

I woke up with a jolt and my hangover hit me. I immediately remembered the incident with Ash, what he had confessed, the fact that I was messing up his ability, that kiss...

What have I done?

I pushed it to the back of my mind, I needed to get ready. Beth had arranged a trip to Lincoln for us, and although I felt awful, I didn't want to disappoint her; she seemed so excited about it.

I had also decided that after we returned home, I would tell them everything. They were risking their lives for me, they should at least know what was going on. Even though I hadn't seen those creatures since the incident in town, I knew this was far from over.

Beth drove us to Lincoln, with me in the passenger seat and Ash sitting quietly in the back seat, half hungover, half embarrassed.

If she noticed an atmosphere, she didn't mention it.

Around an hour and a half later, I woke up with a jolt, unaware that I had been asleep. I scanned my surroundings. We were on a cobbled back street, and I looked over to see Beth huffing in frustration.

"There's never anywhere to park in this place!" she groaned, turning the car around and driving out onto a different street.

"Sorry I fell asleep," I said, yawning.

"It's alright," she replied. "You looked so peaceful; with the drool and everything, I didn't want to wake you."

"I was drooling?" I said in panic, putting a finger to my lips. She giggled.

"No," she answered, smiling. "But there was some snoring." She then gestured to Ash. "And I definitely didn't want to wake him up; he's grumpy enough as it is."

I looked over my shoulder at Ash, whose eyes were closed, a strange half smile on his face. His feet were up and his music was still playing in his ears. But he was dead to the world.

Beth finally found a free space in a car park up a small hill, and we parked up. She woke Ash up but he groaned and rolled over to face away, but then realised that he was in the car and not his bed. He begrudgingly sat up with a yawn and pulled himself out of the car.

I opened my door, and slowly got out, stretching my limbs like a cat. The warm sun hit me, and the cool breeze blew my hair over my shoulders.

We paid for the parking, and then wandered down the hill. We passed various shops and buildings, narrow streets and traditional pubs. We browsed a few book shops, and Beth bought some sweets and chocolate from a very long-established shop; the man who owned it said he had taken over from his father who owned the shop before, and he from his own father.

Beth then led the way up the hill to where a beautiful cathedral was apparently sitting, and when she said there would be a hill, she wasn't wrong.

It was named very aptly "Steep Hill" and there were even more traditional shops and a few pubs. Standing at the bottom, it looked more like a staircase with no stairs, and as we started making our way up, my head pounded and my thighs ached by the time we got halfway. Beth was striding on, not even breaking a sweat, yet Ash and I lagged behind, breathless.

As we walked, I could tell he was about to say something. Part of me never wanted to speak of it again, but we needed to sort this out if we were to continue as friends. Beth was far up ahead, out of earshot.

"Aria," he began. "I am so sorry about last night. For the drawings, the glass...are your cuts okay?"

Neither of us had dared to ask Beth to heal them; it would have invited too many questions.

"I'm fine, don't worry about it," I replied. "And I'm sorry too."

"For what?" he asked.

"For kissing you, I don't think I feel..."

He put a hand up to stop me. He understood. He didn't need to hear the rest of the sentence. I closed my mouth sheepishly.

"Let's not speak of that, ever again," he replied. "Although, if I hadn't have almost cut you to ribbons, I would have *so* been in there, right?"

And with that arrogant, playful remark, the awkward atmosphere was instantly lifted. I smiled at his amused face.

"Not a chance," I replied, smiling. A flicker of sadness washed over him then, but he hid it quickly, and I pretended not to notice.

"There was one thing that worries me though," I then said softly. I wanted to change the subject without it being obvious that that was my intention, but it didn't really work. Ash took the bait though.

"You mean about your ability?" he asked.

"Yeah, I'm worried what I might be doing to others around me."

"Well Aria, we can always sort it out when we get home."

"Thanks," I smiled. He always knew exactly what to say to make me feel better.

He fixed his eyes onto Beth, who we could hardly see anymore.

"I tell you what, she's got some powerful thighs on her, that girl," he said. "Beth! Beth! Wait for us, would you?"

We saw a small figure turn, put her hands on her hips and shake her head at us. We staggered up the rest of the way half leaning on each other.

"Jesus Christ," Ash said, hardly audible between the gulps of air he was trying to fill his lungs with. "Where's this bloody cathedral then?"

"Its just up ahead," Beth replied. She turned on her heel again and power-walked up the street.

"We need to go for a pint after this," Ash commented. "We've walked past loads of pubs, they do food as well."

"Yeah, we'll go for food in a little while," Beth replied. "But I promised I would show Aria the cathedral, and…here it is."

We walked through an archway, and as it ended I saw the bottom of the cathedral, and I slowly worked my eyes up, unable to look at the building as a whole.

My heart thumped hard in my chest and I gasped; I couldn't believe my eyes. The building stretched up high into the sky, its steeples and towers reaching upwards, as if on tiptoes. The intricate detail of the architecture was so perfect; this must have taken hundreds of years to build and sculpt to this detail. I would never have had that kind of patience. I was sure I could see little statues and gargoyles embedded in the grooves of the building, and huge towers came out the top, stretching on even further.

"Wow," I said, unable to think of anything else to say.

"I know," said Beth. She grabbed my arm excitedly. "Shall we look around?"

"Sounds good to me."

I turned to Ash, who was still staring at the sight he saw in front of him.

"That's actually quite impressive," he said. He then turned to us. "Are we going inside?"

"Yes," replied Beth. "But we're just going around the outside first."

We made our way along the path and around the building. It was as long as it was wide. There were more arches, more statues, and I could now see in detail the long, beautiful stained glass windows. It seemed to stretch on forever.

I saw Beth's eyes, full of amazement, trailing over the building. She really had an appreciation for things like this, which was nice because I did too. Ash took out his phone and we stood there for a while, taking pictures. There was one of Ash and me, then Beth and me, then the two of them together.

We asked a passerby to take one of the three of us, and we stood, grinning at the camera, trying to keep still. The passerby handed us the end result with a smirk, and I wondered what was so amusing, but then I chuckled myself as I saw that Ash had strategically managed to put his hand behind Beth's head and stick two fingers up. She looked like she had antennae.

"Ash! You dick!" Beth said, and smacked him on the arm. He just laughed, and put his phone back in his pocket.

"Come on," he said. "Let's go inside."

We made our way to the front of the building. We put our donations in the box in the main reception area, and then stepped through the large, looming wooden doors.

The view took my breath away. Huge stone pillars reached to the ceiling on both sides, forming beautiful archways. There was a long, stone-slabbed corridor with ceilings higher than I had ever seen. Light poured in from the windows, splashing over the entire room, making it bright, almost shining. Rows of pews congregated in the centre of the room, and I saw a few people sat thinking, praying.

I felt as though I had stepped into another world, into a different time, free of the influence of today's society. This building was old, very old, and knowledge and wisdom oozed from every brick and stone. At the back of the room there was a kind of stage, and there were more chairs and a huge organ. Candles flickered, and hushed voices and echoing footsteps filled the room.

"This is amazing," I said, and Beth smiled at me.

"It is, isn't it?" she replied. We explored the building together in silence, reading information and gingerly touching the walls, the statues, the pillars, as though if we handled them too much, they would break or crumble.

"This cathedral is nearly a thousand years old," Ash commented as he read one of the plaques about the building's history.

"I can feel it," I replied, turning to him. I inhaled deeply, smelling the musky, old smell only a building like this could possess. I let the atmosphere of the building seep into me, I opened myself up to its energy.

That was when I sensed something…else. I couldn't put my finger on what it was, but it wasn't pleasant. It was as though something had stepped into the cathedral that shouldn't be there. It was something that wished harm, something dark, that inflicted pain. I looked around, searching for what it could be.

But I couldn't see anything. No, wait…That person, was it a man? Or something else? He was at the other end of the room, and despite its vastness, I could still see him staring at me. His face was pulled into a grimace, he looked almost as though he was in pain. I was shocked at the sight before me. *Who on earth is that? Why is he staring at me?*

He was dressed in normal clothes: a brown jacket, blue jeans, trainers. His hair was a short, neatly trimmed black, and if I couldn't feel such hatred emanating from him, I wouldn't have given him a second glance. I looked over to Ash and Beth. They weren't looking in my direction. I looked back to the man, only to see that he had disappeared. I glanced around, but he was gone. It brought me no relief.

Towards the back of the room, there were dozens of candles lit up, the brightness emanating from the flames lighting up everything around it. There were more candles in a box that weren't lit, and a money box on the left.

"What's that for?" Ash asked, puzzled.

"It's for prayers," Beth replied. "You put a donation in the box, light a candle and make a prayer. Have you never done that before?"

She looked at him, quite bewildered that he had asked her such a question. He stared back at her for a few seconds, preparing his comeback.

"Shut up," he finally mumbled, and she laughed. She then took out a coin from her purse and slid it into the box. She then carefully took a candle and lit it with the flame of another one. Setting the candle into a nearby holder, she knelt down and bowed her head. As she did this, I became quite uncomfortable; I was watching something very private, and I should either join in or leave. I took a candle, and reached over to drop my change in the box.

"We're doing this as well are we then?" Ash whispered to me, a rather disapproving look on his face. I shrugged my shoulders.

"You don't have to if you don't want to," I whispered back, and he stood for a few seconds, thinking it over. He then sighed hard, and reached into his jeans pocket for a coin.

"I suppose it wouldn't hurt," he replied, and although reluctant, he took out a candle, lit it, and then we stood for a few more seconds in silence. I wondered what on earth to pray for, and to whom I should pray. I didn't believe in God, and I knew Ash didn't either, but it seemed a good a time as any to gather my thoughts. I closed my eyes.

Dear…God, or Gods, or spirits, I'm not sure if this is something I usually do, but I need your help. I need my memory back; I need to know who I am, and what happened to me. So any help there would be greatly appreciated. I would also like to thank you for sending Ash and Beth to me. They literally saved my life, please keep them safe. Amen.

I opened my eyes again, and saw Ash kneeling beside Beth, his hands resting on his knees. His lips moved slowly and silently, and I smiled to myself. I wondered what he was praying for. Beth turned back to me first, then Ash did the same, and we then made our way around the rest of the building.

"So what did you wish for?" Ash asked me, a wide grin on his face.

"None of your business," I replied flatly, looking smugly back at him.

"Besides," Beth chimed in, a tone of irritation in her voice. "It's not a wishing well, you don't wish for things. Its prayer, its reflection."

"Same thing," Ash remarked playfully, but then he became silent when I shot him a disapproving look. We should respect Beth's beliefs.

We stayed another hour or so before Ash drove us home, with me in the passenger seat again, and Beth in the back.

It was beginning to get dark, and I watched in wonder as the blue sky turned red, and the clouds glowed a yellowy orange. I could make the faint outline of the waning moon.

Today was a good day; my friends were strong people, with their own minds; and I was grateful for that. We had something in common, and I felt lucky to have them.

The strange man flashed through my mind's eye, but I forced him back. *No, don't ruin this for me, I have only just started getting things back on track again.*

When we got back to the flat, I cleared my throat.

"Guys?" I said. They both turned around. "When you're ready, I want to talk to you about something."

Beth held my arm and stroked it soothingly. "Are you okay?"

"Yeah, I'm fine. I just want to explain to you…some stuff…you should know…"

They exchanged worried glances.

"Okay Aria, whatever you need," Ash replied.

"Okay, good, thank you," I said. "I'm just going to get changed and then we can have a cup of tea or something?"

"Sounds good, I'll make the tea," Ash replied.

I took a nervous breath and then went to my room. *You can do this, you can tell them everything you know. Maybe they could help. You can trust them; they are your friends.*

As I undressed, I heard a loud bang. My heart thundered in my chest as I heard Beth shout something. *What was that?* I grabbed a nightgown and threw it over my head, opening the door. I looked out through the hallway and towards the living room.

Ash and Beth were there, standing over something.

"You guys okay? I heard a noise," I said.

They both looked back at me, shocked for a moment, and then their faces cleared.

"I just dropped something," Beth replied. "Don't worry about it."

"Are you sure? You look startled?" I asked. *Something's weird.*

"Yeah, we're fine. We'll be waiting for you in here when you're ready."

"Alright, see you in a minute then."

I finished preparing myself, mentally more than anything, and then went back to the living room to face them.

CHAPTER TWENTY

Nick

Of all places, we ended up in bloody Lincoln. Why would the shifter bring them here? I kept my distance as they made their way up to the Cathedral. The last time I came here was with Jenny, and as I walked past shops we had gone into and places we had looked upon with awe, I felt a stab of pain. *No, let it go; you have work to do.*

I watched the shifter carefully, and it looked around, amazed at all it saw. I followed them into the cathedral, and it gazed at its surroundings as though seeing it all for the first time. It couldn't have been Jenny then, because we had already been to the cathedral. It was uncanny though, every look of astonishment, every step the shifter took, everything it delicately touched, was the way she did it. It was like watching it all again. But the shifters are very convincing, I knew better than to be tricked by it again. So I just watched, standing in the shadows.

It looked at me once, in a bewildered sort of way, and I maintained eye contact, showing it that I wasn't scared, that I would do to it what I had done to others of its kind. But my heart, when it looked at me with her eyes, my heart pounded, and I had to let them walk out of my line of sight before I was able to breathe again.

I followed them home, still figuring out what my next step should be, my blood sugar levels plummeting as I hadn't eaten all day. When they got back, they just went back into the flat. *What's going on here?*

I stopped by at a Macdonalds drive through, and then went back to Jenny's house.

After lighting another cigarette and finishing off my coke, there was a knock at the door. I opened it, expecting to see another monster wearing the face of my soulmate. But it was the boy, Ash. I blinked in surprise, wondering whether to gut him on my doorstep, or shake his hand and invite him in. *Is he human? Or just another shapeshifter?*

But I didn't have to wonder for long, as he shed his skin on the doorstep, opened his fangs, and went for my throat.

The creature lunged at me, and we both fell back into the house and onto the floor. I cracked the back of my head, and blood began to seep from the wound. Sickeningly, the creature forgot me for a moment as it lapped up the drops of blood that had fallen onto the wooden tiles. Pain shot through my head, my neck, my fingertips, but I stood up shakily and prepared myself for the second blow.

It locked its milky eyes with mine and snarled, and then lunged for me again. Falling back, I reached out for the button I had installed next to the kitchen door, and I kept my back flat against the wall as the trap doors opened just in front of me. The creature fell through them and down to the basement. I ran quickly, my breath catching in my throat, down the basement stairs and I watched as it recovered from the fall and crawled up to the corner of the ceiling, like a spider. It was unnerving.

I pulled out my knife, flicked on the light and stepped down into the basement carefully. Dust floated around in the air; it had been disturbed by the shifter. I tried not to cough when I inhaled the muskiness. I could see it, gripping the wall with its claws, its eyes fixed on the chair that I had used to torture its friends. I hoped that the sight of the dried, blue blood that covered the chair and the floor would instil fear into the shifter, to make it more wary of me.

Holding the knife up as a warning, I spoke.

"How many of you do I have to kill before you give me what I want?" I asked it.

It hissed at me, remaining still, clutching the wall.

"I will kill you," it replied through gritted teeth.

I couldn't help but laugh.

"Seriously? You guys are just cannon fodder. You're being flung at me, to distract me, without any concern for your lives. Your boss doesn't give a shit."

"My life is of no concern to me," it said. "She sends us, and we do as we are instructed. A hundred of us could die, a thousand, and she will make more."

"Make?" I asked.

"You stupid child," it snarled. It crept down from the ceiling and stood up. Its bald, pale head brushed against the ceiling, and my neck started to ache from looking up at it. "You can't stand in the way of us," it continued. "You may as well just let me kill you now."

"Don't think so mate," I replied, and held up the knife high, trying to look as fear inducing as possible.

A flash of light then obscured my vision, and I fell to the floor, the pain in my head excruciating. *Not now, for fuck's sake, not now! Stop! Stop!*

The vision thrust itself into my mind, it was all I could see. But the shifter was still there, in front of me, tall and dark. Then everything went black, as though I had suddenly gone blind. I looked around wildly, clutching my heart. *I'm going to die.*

The room lit up again as though lightning had struck, and

there the shifter was again, but someone else was in the room, on its shoulders, his arms gripped around the shifter. *Mark.*

Everything was once again black, and then a blinding bright, burning my eyes in the process. I saw Mark's fierce determination as he pulled the shifter to the ground, and snapped its neck in one smooth, powerful movement. Then black.

I opened my eyes, blinking against the the brightness of the light bulb in the basement as though it was as searing as the sun. I looked around, the knife ready in my hands, but the shifter was gone. The only thing left was the tell-tale blood, blue and thick, spreading across the dusty basement floor.

Jesus Christ.

"Mark?" I called out tentatively to the empty space around me. *Is he here? Is he alive? This was proof, wasn't it?*

My fingers traced the wound at the back of my head, and anger rose inside me like bile. This was the last time I would sit around waiting to be beaten up. I needed to go back to the flat, to see who – or what – Ash and Beth were. I would take the shifter, and even if it took a month, I would make it tell me everything it knew.

Parking up outside the flat, the sight in the window confirmed everything for me. Shifters, not even bothering to disguise themselves, creeping around the flat. Two of them. *They already know I'm here. They're enticing me in to kill me. We shall see.*

I took out my knife, and approached the building.

CHAPTER TWENTY-ONE

Aria

Ash placed the coffee mug down onto the kitchen table with a smile, and he then handed Beth hers.

"Thanks," I said to him.

He smiled in reply, and we all sat in a tired yet comfortable silence, sipping our drinks. They waited for me to start talking.

Everything that I had learnt over the past few weeks, about them, about myself, it gave me hope, it gave me strength to figure out what part I had to play in what happened at the hospital, and that I wasn't completely alone. I would always have Ash and Beth, even if everyone I knew before had abandoned me, they would always be here; they loved me.

"Okay," I said to them. "So there are a few things I need to tell you…"

A loud bang made me jump. My skin pricked up in fear. *Was it those things? Were they back for me? Why couldn't they just leave me alone?*

I put my mug down, my hands shaking. The bang had come from the living room. Ash and Beth exchanged worried glances, and we all crossed the kitchen threshold and into the hallway. The front door was wide open. *Someone's here.*

"Aria, stay near me," Ash said. I felt him tense beside me, taking his position as the man of the house. "Beth, you too. Back to the kitchen, grab something to defend yourselves."

We moved as one back to the kitchen, and I grabbed a pair of large scissors, clutching it between my hands like a dagger. Ash took out a knife from the drawer. He passed it to Beth, who took it without pause, and Ash then took another knife out for him. Even though we were now armed, it didn't make me any less terrified.

"Should we call the police?" I whispered.

"Just wait a minute," Ash replied. "Okay, you two stay here. I'll take a look."

He stepped out into the corridor. Someone must have been hiding just beyond the doorway, out of sight. Before I could reach out to even warn Ash, a large hand brandishing a knife struck him in the face. The blade sliced up through his jaw, vanishing into his skin, all the way up to the hilt. I screamed. The hand then pulled the blade out, and a large, black boot kicked him backwards.

Ash was dead before he hit the floor. I screamed again. I wasn't sure what I screamed, or how long I screamed for, but I found myself suddenly at his side, shouting, yelling, crying. I picked up his tall frame and shook him violently, but his face was blank, his eyes still wide in shock from the blade. He was dead.

I turned, suddenly feeling an overwhelming fatigue, and stood up to face whoever had intruded into our home. All I could see what a dark figure, tall, looming, the flash of his blade.

Beth, who I had almost forgotten, lunged at him, her knife held high.

"No!" I screamed. "Beth! *No!*"

The figure punched her in the face, knocking her back, before then thrusting the knife into her chest. Nausea consumed me, I was going to be sick, I was going to pass out. *I'm next.*

She fell next to Ash, and flailed around. I looked away, unable to watch as she died. The figure stepped out of the shadows. It was a man, with dark hair, wild eyes. He looked homicidal. I recognised him. He was the man who I had seen in the cathedral only a few hours earlier. He'd followed us here. I had let him follow us to the flat, and now my best friends were dead. *What have I done?*

I grabbed the side of the kitchen worktop to steady myself. Ash and Beth's bodies melted before my eyes, puddling into nothing. Bile rose up from my stomach, and I retched onto the floor where I stood, my head swimming. *I'm going to pass out, I'm going to die here, he's going to murder me.*

In the haze, I saw the man watching them intently, and when their bodies melted into nothing, he smiled. His eyes then darted over to me.

"You." He pointed to me with a large, dirty finger. "You're coming with me."

"No!" I screamed. I held up the scissors that were miraculously still in my hand, and I went to strike him as he walked slowly towards me, but my head wouldn't stop pounding, swimming. The scissors fell from my hand, and just before the floor came up to meet my face, I saw my half finished coffee. It was green…not bright green, but a sludgy, murky kind of swamp green. How did I not notice it before? Before I passed out I had one last thought.

Ash and Beth had poisoned me.

CHAPTER TWENTY-TWO
AUGUST, 2007

Freya

I had spent an hour in one of the dirty, dank cells, with this moron, and I was beginning to lose my patience. All I needed was information, that was all. Why couldn't people be more forthcoming with such things?

He was middle-aged, bald, fat, and he smelt like he'd bathed in sewage. Even though he no longer had use of his limbs, even though I had cut him until he looked like a beautiful patchwork quilt, he still wouldn't talk.

I usually punished anyone who interrupted my torture sessions, but this time it was worth being interrupted for. One of my children gave me the announcement that the friends had been found. The boy and girl. My babies brought them to me, and I saw with delight that they had already been beaten. They were my leverage, my Plan B. Of course, my Plan A to capture Jennifer herself kept failing, stupid girl. All I wanted was what was mine.

I had also been sorely disappointed by the efforts of some of my children in killing the annoying lover, who couldn't seem to keep his nose out of my business. I had sent them over and over to kill him, but instead I find out that he'd made easy killings of them. Making me look like an idiot. It was a simple task, if I could have done it myself I would have. I made a few heads roll that day I can tell you.

So, I couldn't help a smile creep onto my face when Jennifer's accomplices were brought to me. They looked scared, confused, angry. I loved a challenge, and my fingers itched to shed some blood and elicit some screams.

"Thank you, my loves," I said to my children, who nodded and then backed away.

I turned back to my current task. This one had been brought in for questioning on his dealings with a certain relative of mine who had betrayed me. He either didn't know anything, or he knew that if he told and I let him live, he would be dead anyway. I was suddenly bored, and excited at my new task, so I ripped out the man's tongue, and left him in his cell to bleed to death. I had fingers in many pies you see, and my patience wears thin quickly.

I turned to the two children in front of me. They smelt like fear. *Wonderful.* I like it when they fear me.

The boy tried to stand up and face me like the man he wished he was, but I broke both of his legs in one swift kick, and he tumbled to the floor, crying out in agony.

As he continued to writhe, I closed my eyes and swayed to the wonderful cries and shouts. The sound was so sharp, so loud, and the fact that I had created it made it sound all the more beautiful.

When I opened my eyes, I saw that the girl had knelt beside him, trying to comfort him. I could smell her ability from where I stood. She reeked of it. I watched as she held her hands out to heal the boy's legs.

"Try it and I'll have your hands cut off, darling," I spat at her. The boy grabbed her hands, and pushed her away.

"Beth, don't, its okay," he said. *So cute.*

She reluctantly put her hands on her lap, and started to sob.

"Good," I said. "Right, now, your name is Beth. And you're Ash, is that right?" They both nodded. "Good. So you're probably wondering why you're here. All I have is a few questions, and all you need to do it answer them. Understood?"

They both glared at me, menacingly. It was sweet, adorable, but I had to set an example. My children would not be very pleased if I let these two get off lightly.

So I removed their eyes.

Their screams pierced the air, and I let them stew in darkness for a while, whilst my children secured them into place, chaining them against the wall. The girl tried to cry, but with no eyes, it was a curious effort.

"I will only ask this once, understand?" I asked again.

I took their muffled cries as agreement. I gave them back their eyes. They would need them, after all, so they could see what I was going to do to them.

The girl's tears began to fall down her cheeks, and I leant over to her to lick them from her face. She shuddered against my tongue, it was delicious. *Salty fear.*

"Please," she whispered. "Please let us go."

"That will depend entirely upon you, sweetie," I replied. "And this one here." I grabbed the boy's hair and yanked his face up to meet mine. He was trying to lift himself up on his broken legs. I stifled a laugh; I had to be professional about this. There was a fire beneath his eyes, it just needed a bit more to push it out. But he wasn't a threat to me.

"So, where is Jennifer?" I asked.

The boy Ash stopped struggling and looked back at me, perplexed.

"We don't know who that is, you have the wrong people. Please just let us go!" he said.

"You do know," I replied. "She goes by a different name now though. Amnesia, of all silly things. You know her as Aria."

"What do you want with her?" asked Beth. For her cheek, I slapped her across the face. Not too hard, just hard enough to give her a warning.

"I'll be asking the questions, dear," I said. "Now, she should have been here by now, delivered by my children, but I sense that something has gone wrong. Tell me, what was she plotting? Who has helped her escape?"

They looked at each other, scared, confusion clouding their faces. Perhaps they actually didn't know anything, perhaps she never learnt it herself. Nevermind, I could still play with them for a while, before adding them to my ranks.

I began with the girl, her screams were sweeter, and she made a lot of them when I tore into her flesh. Just a few small, shallow cuts to start with, to get the blood flowing. The boy cried out for me to stop, to take him instead of her.

"There is no instead, dear," I replied. "There is only first, and second."

Either they were good, or they genuinely knew nothing, but it was fun nonetheless.

I locked them up in a spare cell I keep for guests, barely conscious, and then I went to see why my babies had not delivered sweet Jennifer.

Time to make some more heads roll.

CHAPTER TWENTY-THREE

Aria

I awoke to a chilled silence, and I opened my eyes to find a thick blanket of darkness washed over me. I couldn't see an inch in front of my face. Something had been placed over my head. *Is it a bag?* The fabric of it itched. My hands were tied behind my back with what felt like metal handcuffs. I was sitting on a chair, to which my legs were tied. The air was hot and thin, I felt like I was about to suffocate.

I pulled and pushed against my restraints, contemplating whether to try and gnaw myself free, when the bag over my head was swiftly pulled off, catching a clump of my hair with it. I screamed as the roots of my hair were ripped out of my head. The man was stood above me, one leg resting on the chair. He was as I remembered – dark features, unkempt appearance, and in his eyes he looked like he was capable of anything. He wore dark jeans and a black jacket, and he stood mockingly, with a stupid grin on his face, smoking a cigarette.

"Those things will kill you, you know," I remarked.

My voice trembled as I said those words, and I cursed my wavering resolve. He laughed, and took another drag before stubbing it out on my bare arm. I screamed again, the pain excruciating.

"*What are you doing?! You bastard! Get away from me!*" I cried. I yelled and yelled for help until my voice was hoarse, and he just sat and watched me.

"Are you finished?" he asked me when I had quietened down. Before I could answer him, he grabbed my face roughly with his dirty fingers.

"What the hell are you doing?!" I cried. "Get off me!"

"What's your name?" he asked me.

"Excuse me? What's your fucking name?" I asked, panic giving a momentary sense of courage.

"Answer me."

"Fuck off."

He grabbed my shoulder, and pulled me forward so forcefully that I felt a sharp twinge shoot through my neck.

"This isn't a game, answer the question."

He pushed my face back and I hit my head on the back of the chair. *Oh God, he's going to kill me.*

"I don't know," I whispered. "I don't know who I am."

To my shame, I began to sob then, uncontrollably. His shaking hands took out another cigarette, and he lit it, and took a long, hard drag.

"You're good," he remarked, weighing me up from where he stood. "But you're not the most convincing I've had." The more he spoke, the more confused I became at his words.

"What are you talking about?" I asked.

"You don't know who you are?" he spat. "What kind of half-arsed cover story is that?"

"Its true," I whispered. "I…I lost my memory."

"Really?! Well that's a first!" He slapped his thigh and took another drag, smiling as he exhaled the plume of smoke.

"You killed my friends," I said to him darkly through my tears. "And for that I'll kill you."

"I've killed many of your friends," he replied. "It doesn't stop you all from coming to me though does it?"

"What?" *Is he insane?*

"You know what's going to happen, don't you?" His face was almost touching my own. His breath was a mixture of alcohol, coffee and smoke. I felt sick. "You're going to tell me where she is, or you are going to die. Slowly."

"Where who is? I don't know what you're talking about!" I screeched. For that comment I received a backhand to the face. It quietened me down.

He then walked a few steps away, and paced the room. I looked around, trying to find a means of escape. I was in a basement. I was still wearing my nightie. The morning light filled the dusty, dank room, and diamonds of dust fell through the air, landing on the cold concrete floor. I realised then that I must have been out cold for a good few hours. What had he done with me in the meantime? My eyes then locked onto something.

She was crying, tied to a chair, her whole body shaking in fright. Her matted hair clung to her dirty face, and I could see marks and cuts on her face and body where she'd been tortured. My heart sank. He'd done this before, he was going to kill me and this other poor girl and there was nothing I could do about it.

The horror of what was about to happen hit me, and I struggled to stay conscious. In my panic I heard myself pleading, screaming, crying to be set free.

"You bastard! Let us go! I'll fucking kill you!" I yelled.

He took another chair and sat between me and the other girl, and looked from me to her, and then back again. He looked as though he was waiting for something.

That was when I noticed that the girl opposite me looked so familiar, it was uncanny. She could have been my double. She looked up at me, and held my gaze with dark, empty eyes. She smiled. It was a dark, sickly smile that made me want to look away, but I couldn't. I could see the cigarette burns on her cheeks, and blood in her hair. I felt it now, the cold, the lack of life. She wasn't what she seemed to be.

"Here's one I found skulking outside the house," he said. "Do you two know each other?"

He then stood up and kicked the girl hard, in the face with his boot. I saw the change immediately. The hair receded, revealing a blue, pale head. Her clothes fell to the floor, and her skin turned an ashen blue. Her facial features fused together, and her limbs became elongated, jutting out at a painful angle.

She wasn't even discernible as a girl anymore, it was featureless, shapeless, and in its creamy eyes I saw that there was no humanity. It spat a blue, florescent liquid onto the floor – its blood – and turned away from the man.

"Oh God…" The words escaped without me wanting them too. What was he going to do with this *thing* in front of me? It was one of those creatures, and now this man had brought me right to it.

I kicked back against the chair, putting as much distance between myself and him as possible, but he was quick, and he pulled me back with ease and then bolted the chair to the ground. I was stuck.

"You think I'm that stupid?" he asked. "For fuck's sake, you lot are hilarious." He let out a long, terrifying laugh before then smacking me again. The force was so hard that I felt my brain reverberate in my skull, and I felt vomit rise to the back of my throat. I swallowed it down, my eyes watering.

But it pushed me over an edge I didn't know was there until that moment. I found strength from somewhere, enough to reach out to the energy outside. There were trees and flowers in the garden, I could smell them, feel their intertwining spirits.

I pulled them in and the green dendrites entered the dark room and filled me up. I could feel their power, their energy moving through me. I gathered up the energy swirling around me, and I spat in his dumbfounded face before I emptied it into him, knocking him off his feet and onto the floor.

I sat, glued to the chair, wondering if he was out cold. When he didn't move, I pulled against the restraints tying down my legs, and after what felt like forever, my legs were free.

My hands shook wildly as I then attempted to prise open the handcuffs. I tried to push them off my wrists, to pull them open with my teeth, but they wouldn't come off, so I lifted myself off the chair, and ran up the stairs, desperately searching for a way out.

I closed the basement door behind me, and ran through the reception room to the front door. It was locked, and so I stumbled into the living room, searching for the keys. I found nothing.

"Come on, come on," I said to myself aloud. "Fucking hell, come on!" The man downstairs probably had the keys, and there was no way I was going back down there again, so I took a large ornament of a dog, that had been sitting on the fireplace with another similar dog beside it, and I raised it above my head.

I prepared to launch the dog through the living room window, tensing my arm muscles, when I froze.

On the windowsill was a picture, the most terrifying picture I had ever seen.

It was me.

I was fuller faced, with long hair, sitting in a garden with her, with the dead woman. Her long, red hair shone in the sunlight caught by the camera, and her bright eyes sparkled as she smiled next to me. We looked happy, as we clutched each other tightly in a warm embrace.

The ornament dog fell from my weakening grasp and I barely noticed as it crashed to the floor, breaking into pieces. I took the photograph, heavy in its silver frame, and I stared at my own face. I looked so different, so carefree; there were no worry lines, no scars, no fear of an unknown enemy.

My fingers traced the contours of the other woman's face, and I could hardly believe this was the woman who I had watched being eaten. I sunk to the floor, the photograph laying in my lap.

"I took that one," I heard a voice behind me say. "We were at the park, it was a Sunday...."

He stood with his hand pressed against his bruised face, and his cold, hard stare was gone. He looked terrified.

"Jenny..."

I gripped the photograph tight against my heart, and stood to face him.

"It can't be you..."

He took a step closer, and I took one back. The shards from the dog crunched underneath my foot. He reached out a hand to me, his eyes wide with a kind of excited fear that looked strange on him. I held the photograph tighter.

"What do you want from me?" I asked. My voice was small against the oppressive silence.

"Do you know who I am?" he asked, taking another step. I shook my head. I could feel my heart pounding like a hammer inside my ribcage, and I hoped that he couldn't sense it.

"This," he looked around, gesturing to our surroundings. "...is your house."

His face was now calm, serene almost, and he stood waiting for my response.

"What?"

"This is your home," he repeated. My body began to sway, and

I fought to stay upright as my mind tried to digest this information. I couldn't think, I was enveloped in a panicked shock. It couldn't be true, it just couldn't. He took another step towards me.

"Get away from me!" I screamed, but he continued to advance. "Get away!"

"I'm Nick," he continued. "I've been looking for you."

CHAPTER TWENTY-FOUR

Freya

I wiped my hands clean of the disgusting blue liquid. I had stained my dress in the process, but I had hundreds of dresses; it wouldn't be too much of a sacrifice. My babies knew the price for a failed mission, they knew what was expected when they disappointed me, and they did make minimal fuss, but still it pained me. Such a waste of my hard work. Still, I could make more, I could make plenty more.

My other children cleaned up the mess, and I went to change my clothes.

Walking past the musty, blood-stained cells, I checked how my new babies were doing. Some were coming along nicely, their human eyes already pale, their skin turning a lovely blue colour, bones enlarging, their minds being wiped. Others however, were taking longer, their minds and bodies were more resilient. They screamed and tried to fight the confines of their cell, but it was a wasted effort; I would get them in the end.

My children had brought me some findings from the hospital a few weeks ago. Not Jennifer unfortunately, who continued to elude me, but others. Some adults, some children, and although they possessed some interesting abilities, they were not as strong as me, and they succumbed to my influence. The last of them, I think she was around seven, she had a strong mind, and she was feisty, she bit and scratched me and tried to run away, but we caught her, and she spent the rest of the transition process in a straight-jacket. A few days later it emerged from the cell; tall, beautiful, powerful, and joined the others. *I'm a lucky mother.*

I finally reached the top of the steps leading up to my room, and unlocked my door. No one was allowed in here, this was my haven, different to the rest of my house, where I could forget that I had actually been trapped here for one hundred and fifty years. Those stupid magic men, those shaman idiots, I would get them eventually.

I thought back painfully on my few failed attempts to leave this place, only to be bound to it even stronger. Well, when I get my power back, when I get what was taken from me, I would be able to leave forever.

I closed the door behind me, and marvelled at my room. It really was beautiful; I felt safe here, serene.

Books ran from one side of the wall all the way to the other end, books about the world, my mentor always stressed the importance of being well read. A large rug made out of real tiger fur caressed my feet as I slipped off my shoes. I was starting to get hard skin on my feet, disgusting. Perhaps this body wasn't as young as she looked.

A large bed lay towards the back. I slept wonderfully there, a globe of the world stood in the centre. At the end was my wardrobe. It was large, filled with beautiful gowns and dresses, sparkling jewellery and diamond studded shoes. Just because I was a prisoner in my own home did not mean that I had to be sloppy and unpresentable.

Of course my room would not be complete without a few pieces I had collected over the years from my battles. Several heads, kept fresh in embalming fluid, adorned the upper walls.

The first head belonged to the only shaman I could ever find that had to do with my interment. The others would now be long gone, but their traditions I had no doubt would still be alive. The next head was of a young soldier who dared to try and 'slay' me like I was some sort of dragon or Medusa. *Silly child.* That one was around seventy years old.

There were a few others, but the two I was most proud of, the two that I had taken because they should have stopped all this nonsense from happening in the first place, were my mother, and my father.

I stood before them all, my porcelain skin now bare, and I smiled. They were reminders of what I was, of what I was taught to be, and if anyone crossed me, well I wasn't being metaphorical when I said I would make heads roll.

I turned and looked at myself in the mirror. The body belonged to a college girl, she was beautiful, pert, a bit of a slut, but that was why I chose her. I took my fingers and tweaked her nipples, watching them harden and pucker. I think she likes that. I turned and jiggled my full, ripe bottom at the mirror and giggled. She was a nice fit actually, I might keep her for a bit longer.

I put on a plain but elegant red silk dress, with matching strappy shoes, and then went back to business.

I had an appointment with two clueless but entertaining individuals.

CHAPTER TWENTY-FIVE

Aria

"Oh, Jenny, I can't believe its actually you! You're here, I thought I would never see you again!" Nick had tears in his eyes, and I saw then how ill he looked. His face was pale and gaunt, his eyes were bloodshot, and he was shaking.

"Please, just let me go, please," I cried. "I want to go home."

He looked at me, confused. "You are home. Jenny, you don't remember me do you?"

All I could do was shake my head. *No, you bastard, I would remember someone as evil as you.*

"Why did you kill my friends?" I asked, my voice hurting from the lump in my throat. "Why?"

"They weren't your friends, Jenny. They were monsters. They were shapeshifters."

"But they looked after me, they took me in and helped me." I sounded whiny, I knew that, but I didn't care.

"They were the same as the creature downstairs. They can shift into any form they like. They weren't your friends Jenny, believe me."

I refused to believe that the people I had been living with, the people that I had grown to love, were out to kill me from the start. It just wasn't possible. Was it?

"They are convincing," he continued. "Very convincing."

I brought a hand up to my face, to wipe away my tears, but I winced in pain from the blow that Nick had given me.

"Oh God, I am so sorry Jenny," he said, his face growing even paler. "I'll get you something."

"I don't want anything from you," I seethed.

He ran to the kitchen anyway and got some ice. I snatched the bag from him and put it to my face. He then went upstairs and came back a few seconds later with some clothes for me.

"Here," he said. "These are yours. Put them on, you must be freezing in just that nightie."

I looked down at myself. I couldn't go anywhere in this shabby thing. I pulled on the jeans and placed the black shirt over my head as Nick turned away.

"Do I have any shoes?" I asked him.

"Over by the front door."

"Thanks." I went over and found some blue trainers. They looked about the right size for me. I put them on.

"Right, I'm going now," I said to him. I couldn't stand to look at his face anymore. "Bye."

I went for the front door. I needed to get help from somewhere, to get my memory back and figure this out. Without this obviously disturbed man.

"Jenny…"

"Stop calling me that!" I said, gritting my teeth. "You don't know me."

He looked wounded, but I didn't care. As far as I was concerned, he had kidnapped me, tortured me, and killed my friends. I didn't want to see him ever again.

"Okay, fine. What's your name?" he asked, his voice light. He was trying to be friends with me.

I answered by slamming the door in his face.

I walked briskly out of the front door, into the sunshine, and down the road. I had no idea where I was, or where I was going, but I just had to get out of that house. All I could think about was that my friends were now dead, and he had killed them. Even if he did know me, it wouldn't change anything. Where was he when I needed him? Why didn't he save me back then? And he wouldn't be able to get my memory back, so I had no use for him.

He hadn't tried to follow me, and around half an hour later, when I had almost reached a small town, I was beginning to feel a bit more hopeful.

I made my way down a small alleyway, shivering despite the warm sun.

A hand grabbed my arm, and I was suddenly spun around on the spot.

"Just leave me alone!" I cried. "Fuck off!"

He had followed me after all. His face was calm, but his hands shook and I could tell by his eyes that he could be volatile, unpredictable. He scared me.

"Please, come back with me, we can sort this out," he said. "Jenny…"

"I fucking told you to stop calling me that!" I yelled. "I swear to God, if you don't get out of my face right now, I'll kill you where you stand!"

He smiled at me then, it wasn't a friendly smile. It was dark; he was inviting me to try. I knew that look. It was the look of challenge. I felt how dangerous he was, I was so close to something that could hurt me, and probably would. *Who is this guy?*

He then started to convulse. His eyes bulged, and his mouth opened. His lips peeled back to reveal the blue skin underneath, and his hair started to fall out. I stepped back. His long, bony hands clutched at the point of a knife that was suddenly protruding from his chest. He then fell, and squirmed about on the floor, before his skin slid off his muscles, and in turn his muscles and bones became goo.

I fell to the floor and vomited, my head pounding. *I can't take this anymore. Please, someone help me, please.*

Stood in the shadows, his knife catching the rays of the sun, was Nick. He'd found me. And he looked pissed off.

"I told you it wasn't safe out here," he said. He helped me up, and I let him, all energy completely leaving my body. "Let's get you home. We have a lot to talk about."

Back at the house, Nick told me my name. I was Jennifer Bailey, I was twenty-four years old, and the last time he had seen me was on the day of the fire. He was Nick Jenkins, twenty-six, and he worked at the psychiatric centre, where apparently I worked too.

"So I wasn't a patient there?" I asked.

"Why would you think that?"

"My memory…it's gone," I said, trying to hold back more tears.

"No, we worked together, I've known you basically all my life. Your mother…the one who was in that room with you, she ran the place. Her name was Laura."

I held onto the photograph again and looked at this woman. She had given birth to me, she gave me life, love, and I couldn't remember any of it. I put down the photograph, exhausted.

"What's going on?" I asked him. "Who are these shapeshifters? What do they want?"

He sighed. "I'm not sure. They want you, that's all I know."

"So I'm special then," I said miserably.

"It appears so."

"So…you took it upon yourself to look for me? Were we that close?" I asked.

He laughed, but it was a bitter laugh.

"I'm your boyfriend," he then said. Deadpan, like he had just said "I'm hungry." Like it was obvious, or normal.

I looked at him, unable to believe that I could be in any way attracted to someone as unhinged as this.

"No you're fucking not," I replied. "No bloody way."

"Seriously?" he asked. "That's really harsh, you know."

"I don't care," I replied. "I've got too much on my plate to be dealing with some psycho boyfriend who's probably been on the scene about three months."

His face was grey, but his eyes were full of pain. I had hurt his feelings, but part of me didn't care. Maybe it was because I was so exhausted, scared, afraid for my life. I didn't want this responsibility too.

"I already told you I've known you for years," he almost spat at me.

"But how long where we together for?" I asked.

"Five of them."

"Five what?"

"Years."

I paused. *Five years?* That was a long time.

"Oh," I said, suddenly embarrassed. Why would I go out with someone who was obviously one cigarette away from emphysema, and who enjoyed beating people up? Did I have that much bad taste?

"Oh indeed," he replied. He then got up, lit a cigarette, and made his way back down to the basement. He slammed the door behind him.

It wasn't long before I heard the screams of the shapeshifter that was still downstairs. He was torturing it right now. I stayed on the sofa, with my knees under my chin. *What do I do now?*

The screams soon died down, and I knew the creature was dead.

CHAPTER TWENTY-SIX

Freya

"Don't hurt her!" the boy screamed. "Please!"

I ignored his whimpering pleas as I sliced into the girl. She yelled and trembled against the knife. She was crying again. It had ceased to amuse me; it was more annoying than anything.

"I told you, silly girl," I said to her. "Look at me. *Look at me.* Good. Do you understand what I mean? Then why did you do it? You must have known what was going to happen."

Behind me, the boy continued to yell and fight against his restraints. There wasn't a scratch on him today, because the girl had undone all my beautiful work. But her powers didn't seem to extend to her own body. She could heal anyone, it seemed, except herself.

I felt a ripple of power then, something on the back of my neck. *Heat. Scorching heat.*

I spun around to face the boy.

"What exactly are you trying to do? Give me sunburn? You're weak and you know it. Especially here. Now sit and wait your turn."

I glared at him until he finally tore away from my gaze. He would never be strong enough to hurt me, not even with years of practice. And he wouldn't have that, I wouldn't give it to him.

But once again, whilst I was carving a lovely piece of skin from the girl's stomach, I felt the heat. It blew against my skin, and a layer of sweat actually formed on my upper lip. He would ruin my makeup, for God's sake. It was distracting. I pulled away the girl's skin, a strip of around three inches, and flung it to the floor.

My children were waiting for scraps, and they fought for each morsel I gave them, like scavengers.

I decided enough was enough.

"Right." I put down my knife, and turned back to the boy. My babies had strung him up on the opposite wall, and I could see that heat, that fire, bubbling up from beneath his eyes. He would make an excellent addition.

"Get away from me!" he yelled. "I'm going to fucking kill you! I'll burn you inside out!"

A laugh erupted from deep inside my gut. *This guy cannot be serious!* He had no idea who he was talking to, the extent of my power. Didn't he know he was already dead?

"Shut up," I replied softly. He smelt hot, like hot air, sweat and must. I could smell his panic, his fear. I held his face and put my lips to his. My mouth muffled his screams, and I exhaled, letting out a formula that had been perfected over a hundred years. I kept my lips against his until he had swallowed everything. When he quietened, and his limbs went limp against the shackles, I pulled away. He was out cold, his eyes closed.

The girl was screaming behind me, screaming the boy's name, over and over. I stood back, and watched what I knew would happen. It would only be a matter of a few days now, perhaps a week, and the change would be complete. She continued to scream, and finally he stirred.

Blinking his eyes, he lifted his neck slowly, and looked at the girl. She shrank back in horror at what she saw. His eyes were now a beautiful milky white, which doesn't always happen straight away. I was glad it did; I wanted to scare the stupid bitch.

As he stared, his expression completely blank, his face twitched into a smile. *Wonderful. Beautiful, my darling.*

I kissed the top of his head before I continued with the girl. He remained there, milky-eyed, smiling all the way through her torture session. In all probability he could still see beneath those eyes, he could see everything I was doing, but his body was no longer his.

It was mine.

CHAPTER TWENTY-SEVEN

Aria

I woke up the next morning to a low, grunting, guttural sound, emanating from one of the doors downstairs. I had slept fitfully on the sofa the night before, despite Nick's efforts to make me sleep upstairs. I didn't want to, I wasn't sure why. Perhaps it was because down here, I was closer to the front door, incase he tried to kill me again.

I thought then back to Ash and Beth. They had been shapeshifters, they had tricked me, and tried to poison me. If Nick hadn't shown up when he did, I would probably be dead now. But had they been shifters all along? They were the only friends I had. And the willow tree, it trusted them. I suddenly felt very alone, and very stupid. They had tricked me, just like they had tricked Nick.

What is that noise? The grunting was then followed by a dull thudding that stopped momentarily and then started up again. I sat up.

Nick was gone, and so I followed the sound through. Just beyond the room was another door, and I could see movement inside it. I stepped closer, and peered through a crack in the door. Nick was pounding on a punch-bag, his hair a sweaty mess sticking out at all angles. He was breathing so hard that he was almost panting, and he had the same look of cold, determined hatred on his face that he wore when he was laying into the shifter.

"You want me to paint that blue for you?" I asked. He turned in surprise and narrowly missed being head-butted by the foam-padded enemy.

"Nah, its alright," he smiled, wiping beads of sweat from his forehead. "But you can go and put on 'Eye of the Tiger' if you like?"

"Eye of the what now?"

"Nothing, nevermind. Its just something you used to mock me with. It doesn't matter."

"Right, sorry," I said.

"Don't worry" he replied. He took off his boxing gloves. "Right, I'm off for a shower. Help yourself to whatever's in the fridge."

He side stepped around me awkwardly and jogged upstairs to the bathroom. Things were still tense between us, mainly because I still didn't quite trust him, and I think I hurt his feelings. But there were more important things to worry about. Food being one of them.

I made my way to the kitchen, walking rather day-dreamily through the living room as I did so. The kitchen was large, with a breakfast table and two red stools, a huge cooker and hob, and around five sets of drawers and cabinets. There was a space underneath the worktop where a washing machine and a dishwasher inhabited, and to the left there was a fridge freezer. The place was quite pristine, and I decided that Nick must either be a clean freak, or that he didn't cook much. The lack of food in the fridge or in any of the cupboards confirmed the latter. All I found was a crate of beer, a clove of garlic and mouldy cheese.

On the plus side, he did have tea and coffee. It was too strange to think about this place as once being mine, mine and Laura's, so I pushed the thoughts back, locking them away until I was ready to deal with them.

I made two mugs of coffee, and sat on the sofa waiting for Nick to come back downstairs.

When he had sat down, I gave him the mug. He smelled fresh, his hair still damp from the shower. I noticed then that his arms were peppered with marks and cuts. New ones. He must have had a rough few weeks.

"Thanks," he replied. "Are you my friend today then?" He raised an eyebrow at me, and I gave him a withering look.

"Just drink your coffee," I muttered. "We have work to do."

"I'll agree with that," he replied, and took a sip. He put the mug back down. "I think I'm going to make mine Irish," he said.

"Seriously? It's half ten in the morning," I said, bewildered.

He gave me a smile that didn't quite suit him; he didn't strike me as the kind to smile very often. It was somewhat forced.

"It's 6pm somewhere," he replied, and went to the kitchen. He brought back a half drank bottle of Jim Beam. He poured a generous amount into his mug, the coffee now looked filmy and almost overflowed out of the mug.

"Want some?" he asked. I could smell it from here.

"God, no. Thanks."

He drank it quickly, and placed the mug back down as though he had just drank a shot at a bar. *This guy has some serious issues.*

"Do you think any more shifters will come?" I asked.

"Most likely."

"So what should we do?"

He sighed. He took out a pack of cigarettes from his trousers, and took one out.

"Do you want one?" he asked.

I looked at him, disgusted. "No."

"Do you mind if I have one?"

"Yes."

He studied my face for a few seconds, before leaning back and lighting one anyway. *Twat.*

"So," I repeated. "What do we do? What's the next step?"

"I really don't know," he answered. "We just need to figure out what they want, who their boss is. Where they come from. But I've spent weeks interrogating them and it's been mostly useless."

"Do you think they had anything to do with my memory?" I asked.

"Possible, but why? Why would they bother?" Nick replied.

I just shrugged; it didn't make much sense.

"Do you know anyone else that might have done this?"

"No, no one," Nick replied. He took another drag of his cigarette. I tried not to breathe in the fumes too deeply. "Unless…" He stopped then, and never finished his sentence.

"Unless what?" I asked, my patience wearing thin.

He turned to me, as though he had forgotten I was there.

"Hmm? What?"

"What were you going to say?" *For fuck's sake.*

"Laura…"

Laura, the woman who was apparently my mother. "What about her?"

"She…she had the ability to erase memories."

My eyes widened in horror. That was it, that was the answer. *She* had done this to me.

He knew what he was saying, and he put a hand up to try and stop me from drawing the most obvious conclusion.

"But she wouldn't," he continued. "She wouldn't ever do that to you."

"You don't know that, Nick. You barely know anything that's going on."

My heart sank as I realised that if Laura did take my memory, it would have died with her.

"I'm telling you she wouldn't, she loved you."

"But it makes sense…"

"Enough!"

Nick slammed his fist down onto the coffee table, suddenly furious with me. He stared at me, his face red. He looked at me the way someone would look at a person they hated, or someone that they were disgusted by. That was the end of the conversation. He got up and left the house, slamming the door. I knew he wouldn't go far, so I didn't go after him.

I sobbed until my throat was hoarse. I just wanted answers, I didn't care where they came from, I just desperately wanted to know what happened to us.

CHAPTER TWENTY-EIGHT

Freya

Well, I had to admit that they were good. They provided a lot of entertainment for me, whilst remaining loyal to Jennifer. It was commendable. But also of no use to me.

The girl Beth was especially fun, as I had grown a preference for girls in recent years, hence the new body.

As I cut out her soft, warm flesh, I lapped up the blood that trickled down her skin. I liked to do this whilst she was naked, it made the sessions all the more thrilling. I had been a while since I had taken a lover, and licking up the spots of blood that dribbled over her breasts, I felt that sweet desire come to me again. Perhaps if she lives through this, I won't turn her, I'll keep her for myself.

The boy, however, was coming along nicely. I sat him up, propped against the wall, as I worked on her. I didn't get the sense that these two had been intimate sexually, but they had a deep bond. So as he watched, I smiled at his trembling lip and milky tears.

I left her to breathe for a few moments, and knelt down next to him.

"Oh dear," I whispered. "You're not much of a man, are you? I mean you couldn't protect this one here." I pointed to Beth. "Look, all you can do it sit and watch, and cry. It's pathetic."

His breathing turned laboured, deep, and I could see his jaw bone working under his skin. His hands trembled. He was angry. I grabbed his face.

"You're so cute," I said. "Let's see what you've got in there."

Leaning my forehead against his hot, clammy face, I closed my eyes. Memories, feelings, thoughts, opinions, fears, hopes, dreams. I could see it all in a person when I wanted to. I used to be able to do more, but the years of imprisonment had been sapping my energy for decades.

Ever since those shamans trapped me here, a piece of me had been missing. They took from me what they thought was all my power, but it wasn't. It was enough, however, to weaken me, to make me angry, and that was the last thing they wanted to do.

I hadn't known where they put my power until twenty-five years ago, when Jennifer was conceived. It seemed that they had hid part of my power in the future, inside a baby. *Idiots. I wonder who came up with that stupid plan.* Didn't they know that I would outlive them all?

The amount of times I almost had her too, and she slipped from my grasp. Her stupid mother, who had eluded us all these years after we tried to take Jennifer as an infant, well…all I can say is I watched my babies eat her with a happiness I had not felt in years.

When I finally get that missing piece from Jennifer, I'll be free, and my vengeance will not only be sweet, it will be dripping with flesh and body parts.

Flashes of childhood, a hot, searing feeling on my back, resentment, unhappiness. This boy had tried to kill himself, stupid child, and in the hospital he had met the girl. Was there any romance here? No…it was a deep friendship. *Sweet.* In fact, this boy actually had romantic, sexual feelings for Jennifer. Despite the fact that I wanted to wrap my fingers around her throat and squeeze until she was dead, I didn't underestimate her. She was too much of a strong, powerful girl to go for a limp dick like this. I mean, what chance could he possibly have?

I withdrew myself from his thoughts.

"She'll never love you the way you love her, you know," I whispered into his ear. "She's far too good for you."

He couldn't turn his head to look at me, but I knew he heard every word.

In his opaque eyes I could still see that fire, but once again it was too weak to be of any threat to me.

"And my, how much she's been *fucked*," I continued. "Fucked by real men, men who know what they're doing. Not you, you could never satisfy her. Not with this." I grabbed the meagre offering he had between his legs, through his blood stained trousers.

"You're a boy, not a man," I said. I let him go. "Now boy, here's a lesson for you."

I returned to Beth, who was still whimpering against the wall, and kissed her roughly, deeply, using my tongue. She tried to squirm away, but she was stuck. I traced her breasts with my hands, felt the hard nipples, and then parted her legs.

She begged me to stop. I wished then, for the purpose of this session, I'd been in a man's body.

I had spent around forty years as a man, and I fucked, my God I fucked so many girls. I built up a name for myself, and at one point, women came to me, flocked to me like dogs on heat, and I fucked them all.

But then the shamans had caught up with me again, and imprisoned me back to this dank, depressing place. And of course I lost my body, so I had to find a new one.

But, I'd had my fair share of women too, and when my babies brought me a specimen to devour, despite their cries and pleas for me to stop, to set them free, they died with a smile on their face and cum between their legs.

It wasn't long before I grew bored with Beth, bored of torturing her, bored of tasting her, and so I kissed her, the way I had kissed the boy, and transferred the essence to begin the process of extraction.

CHAPTER TWENTY-NINE

Aria

As I waited for Nick to return, I decided to rummage around in the living room, and it wasn't long before I found some photo albums. I pulled the first one out of the drawer, knowing what was inside, my heart pounding as I opened it.

Looking back at me, was an old photograph of Laura. She looked so young, her hair a fierce red. She blew a kiss to the camera, and the shot had been taken just as she had blown it from her palm.

I turned the page, and there were four photos of a baby, pristinely stuck into the album with care. I knew in an instant that it was me. In all four of them I was dressed in a pink all-in-one, and I was smiling at the camera, my baby hands trying to reach out to grab it. Dark tufts of hair grew from my head in soft waves, and my eyes sparkled. I looked happy.

Over the page there was more of the same. Me and Laura in the bath, in the garden, in different room of this house, my house. It was Christmas and Laura had piled up an array of presents on the sofa, and I, too young to know what they were, gazed at them in wonder.

"Oh, God," I whispered aloud, tears pooling in my eyes. "What's happening to me? What did I do to deserve this? I want to remember her, I want to remember." I wiped away drops of tears from the photos, and tried to stop a panic attack rising up from my stomach. I closed my eyes, and breathed. In, out, in out.

Just breathe. You can do this. You need to do this. This is your life, you can't ignore it. Do I try and be this person again? Do I try and be Jenny? Or do I carry on as Aria?

I felt as though I had ruined Nick's expectations of me. He had fought for so long, trying to find me, going through all the horrors he had gone through, only to find that the person he knew was gone, replaced by something that wore her face but wasn't her. I was more like those shifters than I originally thought. An empty husk, masquerading as somebody I wasn't.

Nick opened the door and shut it again with a weary sigh. He'd been gone for around an hour. I could tell by his cheeks that he had been crying. I didn't mention it though, I doubted that he would have thanked me for it.

"You alright?" I asked.

"Yeah, fine," he replied. "Look, I'm sorry about earlier."

"Me too," I said. I really was sorry; he was the only person willing to help me, and I needed to trust him more. *But you trusted Ash and Beth, and look how that turned out.*

"If this is going to work," he said. "If we are going to figure this out, you need to start trusting me, you need to start being less of a pain in the arse."

I couldn't help but smile then. "Okay, I'm sorry, I'll try."

"Good. And I mean it, because there's only so much I can take before I boot you out of the front door." He said this playfully, with a brightness in his usually dull eyes.

"No problem."

"Good. Now, I've thought about it, and I think, now that we aren't currently fighting for our lives, we should practice."

"Practice?"

His eyes twinkled excitedly. "Practice."

* * *

"So what do you know about your power?"

Nick looked at me expectantly, waiting for my reply. I sat on the floor of his gym, my legs crossed and my arms sitting lazily in my lap. I had changed into plain black trousers and a dark yellow jumper, borrowed from Laura's wardrobe. It was a little surreal sifting through her clothes, a bit mercenary for my liking, but it was either that or wear Nick's clothes, and I fancied the idea of that even less. I knew that my clothes were in the house somewhere, but I just couldn't face my bedroom yet. I felt stupid that I couldn't just walk in and take what was mine, but the thought of it made me dizzy. I inhaled a fresh, powdery smell that unnerved me, because I knew, even though I couldn't remember it, that this was what she used to smell like.

"Erm, not much really," I replied. "I feel a connection to nature, there's this strange energy, I don't know where it comes from or what it is though."

Nick looked at me and I could see the disappointment in his eyes. I knew what that meant. Jenny knew exactly what her abilities were, and she'd probably perfected them, and could conjure them at will. Second rate Aria on the other hand, was just not good enough.

I looked away, pretending to inspect the small room, complete with punch-bag, weights in the corner, a treadmill and a bike machine. I hoped my ingenuine interest in these objects would steer him away from scrutinising me, but I felt the burning glare of his questioning eyes, and once again I was compelled to meet his gaze.

"Well, I can teach you," he offered, his face no longer holding such pity. "You might even find it quite easy, as you know this stuff already, somewhere in there."

"Okay," I said, and I sat straighter on the floor. Nick was standing by the door, and he leaned against its frame whilst instructing me.

I wanted to be good at this, to pass all his tests, to prove that I was, indeed, worthy of possessing such abilities, and that it would take more than amnesia to make me forget how to use them. Basically, I had tried too hard, and set myself up for failure.

CHAPTER THIRTY

Freya

I woke up with a jolt, my mind hazy. *Where am I? Who's bedroom am I in? Oh God, I've been date raped! Wait…no, this is a girl's bedroom. How hungover am I?*

I sat up in the huge bed. I was surrounded by throws and pillows, the bed itself felt like a large, pink sea. The last thing I remember…I was in a club, there was this handsome guy…I went somewhere with him, and…

I couldn't remember. Was this *his* bedroom, after all? Did I sleep with him?

I stood up, my legs shaking so hard that I had to lean on the wall for support. I looked around.

"Hello?" I called. *What was the guy's name?* "Guy? Hello?"

I looked down at myself. *What the fuck am I wearing? Some frilly pink shit?* My hair was longer, my toenails were a different colour to last night. *What?*

The room was large, filled with books and trinkets, clothes, shoes…high heels…this was definitely a woman's room. I looked up. Around three seconds later I vomited so heavily and so intensely that I actually fell over. Heads, there severed *heads* on the wall. *It's coming back to me. A woman…no, not a woman. Something else…Freya.*

"No!" I shrieked. "No! No!" I banged my fists against the wall. I remembered everything. I remembered *everything*. I remembered torturing all those poor people, doing…awful,

140

disgusting things to them. Only it wasn't me, I swear to God it wasn't me. *It was her.*

I heard her laughing now, laughing at me. No, wait… The laughs were coming from my mouth, but it was her voice. She was still inside me. I needed to get out. I needed to get *her* out.

I screamed and threw myself at the bedroom door. It opened, and I was presented with a long, dark hallway.

I ran forwards into the darkness, hoping to find someone who could help me, who I could help back. But I knew, because I had been there, that all the people currently held in the cells were beyond help. She did something to them, changed them somehow. Would she do that to me? Eventually?

The thought brought a renewed panic up from inside, and I was sick again, my stomach burned. I could taste the sharp tang of blood, and I almost fainted at the thought that not all of it was my own.

I…she laughed again, using my mouth. I ran down another corridor and came face to face with those weird creatures. I screamed again, and prepared myself for an attack, but they merely stepped out of my way. I brushed past them, shivering in fright, and carried on through a door, out through another hallway. *Where the hell is the exit?!*

"Please!" I yelled. "Please let me out! Please!"

I turned another corner, and met a brick wall, turning around I went the other way, and came across a heap of mutilated bodies. *Oh God, I remember each scream, each plea for help, and I just carried on.* I looked at my own hands. I did this. I killed all these people. How can I live with that?

There was no way out. Even if I escaped, she would still be inside me. No way, except one.

I took a sharp looking instrument, still wet and slick with

blood, one of her torture devices. I held it up, and didn't hesitate to bring it down on my exposed throat. Only, my hand wouldn't move. She was holding onto it. She made me drop the implement, and she slapped me across the face.

I couldn't help but weep; I couldn't even kill myself. It was hopeless, I was stuck here, with this evil bitch.

"Oh, I'm not that bad am I?" I asked. She said nothing. Of course she said nothing, because I had gained control again.

"Anyway, enough horsing around," I said. "I believe I have a package coming my way."

CHAPTER THIRTY-ONE

Aria

"You're trying too hard," he whispered from the doorway, and even though I had my eyes closed, I could still feel his unforgiving stare.

"Trying too hard?" I sighed. "How can I possibly be doing that?"

I sat, my hands now resting on my knees, trying to pull the green tendrils of energy that came pouring through the windows from outside, into my pathetic self. They quivered like jelly before me, glistening in the light. I was too agitated, and I couldn't concentrate with Nick nagging me to do better.

"You just need to relax a little more," he sighed impatiently. My eyes flew open and I shot him a disdainful look. Nick then huffed at me. "Just...keep trying."

I closed my eyes again and tried to ignore the sweat trickling into my eyes. I'd been *trying* for the past three hours. The energy wouldn't come; I wasn't strong enough. In my last attempt to grab the energy and pull it to me, I watched in frustration as it trickled back out the window. I was usually better than this.

"Can we have a break?" I asked as I stood up with exasperation. Nick nodded wearily in agreement.

"I need a smoke anyway," he said, and went to the kitchen to retrieve his cigarettes. I leaned against the wall and breathed slowly, trying to loosen my tight muscles. My back ached from sitting down for so long, and it felt good to stretch it. I then followed Nick to the kitchen and drank a glass of water as he smoked. I noticed the plant pots on the kitchen windowsill, and I could see the energy coursing through their tiny bodies.

I concentrated, noting that Nick was looking straight ahead out the window, his brow furrowed in deep thought. I wondered if I could get his attention. The tiny stalks of the flowers shimmered in the sunlight; they drank it up. It made them so much stronger. I reached out a hand and very slowly, their faces turned to me, their curiosity suddenly more compelling than their hunger for the sun's rays. Our energies touched in one smooth, fluid motion, and I drew their energy into me, filling me up.

Even though I took it out of them, they did not weaken. The sun was still shining down and they could still receive energy from the garden outside, from me and even from Nick. It was strange; this energy seemed endless, never running out, there was always more, and then it occurred to me that perhaps it wasn't the collective energies of all living things, but instead, one single thread of energy, flowing in, out and through everything, occasionally parting, but always connecting again.

Perhaps it was like the link between the tides and the moon, to-ing and fro-ing, pushing and pulling, rather than giving and taking away.

Nick finished his cigarette, and stubbed it out into the ashtray without taking his eyes off the view outside. I hadn't seen it but I could feel a green garden, full of growing flowers and herbs, and a few trees at the bottom, the wind energising their leaves and branches. Nick then turned to me, not noticing that the flowers in the plant pots had already done the same.

"We should practice outside," he announced.

"You read my mind," I replied with an excited smile. We

headed for Laura's back garden. Just as I exited through the back door of the kitchen, I turned to see the flowers on the windowsill craning their heads back to face the brilliance of the sun.

Nick and I sat on the ground in the grass of Laura's back lawn. The garden itself was beautiful, if a little overgrown now, but nonetheless teeming with life. I spotted an old wooden bench towards the back, beaten by the elements, only a little of its original green paint-work showing through. It sat on a patio, with stars, suns and moons detailing the stone slabs. I turned back to Nick, who was watching me intently.

"Do you recognise anything?" he asked. I looked around once more and even though this was a beautiful garden, I had never seen it before. I shook my head. "Okay, not to worry," he said. "Shall we begin?"

"Yes," I replied. "This is such a nicer place to do this."

"I used to find you here a lot, walking around, sometimes at all hours of the night. You once told me that it relaxed you when you were stressed." He paused. "Are you sure you don't remember anything like that?"

"Yes, I'm sure," I replied. I didn't bother to look around again; there was nothing here that I remembered.

"Okay, so just…"

"Relax, yes, I know."

I loosened up my shoulders and tried to concentrate. I closed my eyes again and I felt the heaving of the whole garden. It lit up in brilliant colours, colours that I couldn't see with my eyes. I felt them: blues, yellows, purples, reds, greens. It was everywhere. I could even feel Nick's energy at that moment, just like the day at the windowsill, and the dying man. He was tired, I felt that emanating from him, and I could also feel that he didn't quite trust me completely, not yet. It was flecked with the deep, rich purple that I saw inside the couple in love, and despite myself I blushed at the thought. I opened one eye to see him staring at me, transfixed.

"What's wrong?" he asked.

"I think…" I sighed. "I think it might be better if you were… away."

Nick stood up, and took a few paces back.

"Like here?"

"Err….more like back in the house, you're a bit off-putting." We exchanged glances, and I saw his lips curl into an involuntary smile. It made me smile too.

"Alright then," he laughed. "Sorry."

"It's okay, nothing personal."

"Well, I'll be inside if you need me."

"Okay." I watched him leave, and I observed that although he looked rather dishevelled, he carried himself with purpose and determination.

When he left me, I instantly became calmer. I laid on my back in the grass. The sun was high now, and its rays hit me like a warm embrace, and I breathed deeply, taking it all in. It came easily. I pulled the energy into my body, and felt the high it gave me as it coursed through my veins.

I stayed in the garden for an hour, basking, I guess any neighbours who might have seen me would assume I was sunbathing on a lovely day. Much more inconspicuous than Nick's sitting-on-the-floor-cross-legged idea. The only reason that I got up at all was because Nick had made me a mug of tea and a cheese sandwich, and we sat together on the wooden bench to eat, more comfortable in each other's company than we had been up until then.

Nick woke me up the next morning by throwing open the curtains and letting the sun almost burn my retinas through my closed eyes. I groaned and tried to get back into the dream I was having. Ash, Beth and I were all sunbathing but for some reason Beth and I were dressed in blue frocks and Ash was wearing a black suit and tie. Instead of towels laying on the sand, we had large beds decorated with soft pillows.

"Wake up," Nick said without a hint of softness or sympathy. "It's getting late."

"Why, what time is it?"

"8.30am."

"8.30? Jesus Christ…" I rolled over and pulled the covers over my head. I snuggled back into the warm darkness and tried to ignore Nick's impatient breathing. In the next instant I felt the covers fly off me, and I sat up and turned to Nick in shock. He was holding the quilt tightly with his fist, as still as a statue.

"What the hell are you doing?" I asked, annoyed he'd woken me up so rudely. "What happened to bringing me a cup of tea or a gentle shake on the shoulder? Where am I, bootcamp?"

Nick stood frozen to the spot, and he was wringing the quilt as though it was wet. He eventually threw it back to me, and I covered myself up again.

"Sorry, I forgot," he mumbled, turning away from me.

"Forgot what?" I asked, but as the question came out of my mouth I knew. He'd forgotten that I wasn't Jenny, and perhaps my reaction to what he did wasn't the same as how Jenny would have reacted. My anger dissipated, and when he didn't say anything back I tried to make amends.

"Sorry, I'll get dressed," I said.

"I'll get you that tea," said Nick.

He then left, and I searched the bedroom floor for my clothes.

Nick had showed me the rest of the house the evening before, and it was beautiful. There were three bedrooms, one of them was mine, one was Laura's and one was spare, all neatly kept. The furniture was old, un-matching, but they gave the rooms character.

I had stood at the closed door of my bedroom, and I willed myself to go in. I just needed to get it over with. I took a breath, held the door knob tightly, and pushed down. It clicked open and swung out slowly. Here it was, everything that was me, and it turned out to not be that bad. I sat in my old room for an hour that night, and went through everything I could stand to go through.

There was a dressing table with various make-up bits, hair products and nail varnishes. I picked up a dark purple nail varnish that I recognised to be the last one I had painted my toenails with before that awful night. There were a few teddies scattered around the room, anonymous. They should have meant something to me; they should all have their unique stories of how I got them, but they could have belonged to anyone.

The one good thing that I was really grateful of however, was that I got all my clothes back. I went through the countless tops, jewellery, shoes, and tried everything on. A few things I decided should be thrown away, like a bright orange sequinned dress that made me look like a traffic cone, and a few tops that didn't fit me anymore. I found some pale blue cotton pyjamas in a drawer, and that's what I had decided to wear for bed. But I couldn't sleep in my room, it freaked me out a bit, so I slept in Laura's. Her smell was everywhere.

I took some black jeans and a plain green top to Laura's bedroom before I went to sleep along with a beautiful black laced bra and matching thong I found in my underwear drawer, and I couldn't wait to try them on. I fumbled around in the bed, reaching down to pick up my clothes, and I stood by a long mirror Laura had on the inside of one of her wardrobes and put on the matching underwear. It had been so long since I had felt sexy, and I revelled in it for a few minutes before putting on the rest of my clothes and meeting Nick downstairs. He'd made my tea, which he left on the kitchen worktop, whilst he buttered some toast.

"Thanks," I said. I took a seat on one of the kitchen stools. "So what's the plan for today?"

"Well," Nick replied. "You know that thing you did the other day, in the basement?"

"Thing?"

"When you threw that energy at me? We'll, I've never seen you use the energy quite like that before. To use against someone I mean, for self-defence. I thought we could see where it could lead." He slid over a plate of two slices of toast over to me. "Now eat up, we've got work to do."

"Sir, yes Sir," I chuckled, and Nick gave me a sideways glance at my sarcasm before sitting down to eat his own toast.

After breakfast, we went to Nick's makeshift gym room. I didn't know what he expected of me, I'd never had any kind of self defence training, or if I did, surely he wouldn't assume that I would remember it. I felt a bit silly even contemplating a sparring session with him; I wouldn't get very far. Nick took his boxing gloves and handed them to me.

"Put them on," he said. I looked at him quizzically.

"Seriously?" I asked. "I've never done this before."

"No time like the present," he replied. I took them reluctantly and put them on, feeling even more ridiculous. He saw my sour face, and laughed. "Oh come on, its not that bad, I do this all the time."

"But I don't know what I'm doing."

"I don't expect you to Aria, but there will, at some point, be more shifters, and I want you to be able to defend yourself. If anything happened to you…I'm just not taking no for an answer, okay?"

"Fine," I sighed. "But you can't laugh at me for being crap."

"I'll promise that I'll try not to laugh," he smiled. "Right, lets see how you punch. Try and hit the punchbag." I looked from Nick to the punchbag and then back again, perplexed.

"Err… I'm not going to hit that."

"Why not?" Nick was beginning to grow irritated with me, but I just couldn't see the point. I wanted to be able to defend myself against the shifters, but I didn't think this was the way. The punch-bag was large, red and inanimate, and I wouldn't be wearing boxing gloves when the shifters decided to drop by. It just wasn't realistic. I wanted to learn about my ability.

"Alright," Nick sighed. "Let's try something else." He took off the boxing gloves and put them on the floor in the corner. "Do you have any ideas?"

I thought for a few seconds and I was struck by an idea that, at the time, I was rather proud of. In hindsight my common sense should have stopped me. I ran to the kitchen to retrieve some soup cans, cans of tinned tomatoes and tins of baked beans, and brought them back to the gym. I then got some paper and a pen, and drew some menacing faces. Nick watched me, baffled, and he then laughed when I stuck the menacing faces to the tinned goods and lined them up on a table near the back wall.

"There," I said, trying to rub ink off my fingers. "Now we have something to work with." I ignored his chuckling.

"Love the drawings," Nick drawled as he composed himself. "Now what do you propose to do with them?"

I sat on the floor facing the tins, and Nick stood back, out of my view. I then closed my eyes and concentrated, pulling the energy from the garden into my fingertips. I imagined the shifters, their pale expressionless faces, their tall figures and long limbs. They were terrifying. The energy hummed inside me, and when I was ready I opened my eyes and threw it as hard as I could.

The green, glittering ball only flew past the cans, and out the window, being swallowed up again by the earth. I tried again, and I was grateful that Nick had kept silent so far. I imagined Laura, and all those people who died that night, and that these shifters were hunting Nick and me. I was energised yet calm, with a clear focus. I sent the second ball of energy hurtling towards a can of beans. I collected another ball quickly and threw it. It smashed into the tinned tomatoes and the soups, and another one finished off some ravioli.

I then stopped, exhausted, and viewed the damage. The tins were in bits on the floor, and the various contents of them were also on the floor, as well as the walls, and red specks of sauce spotted the ceiling.

"Ah," I said, standing up. Nick came forward and took a look at the mess.

"Well done, I guess," he smiled. He picked up a now smouldering can of soup and examined it. It was as though it had exploded, as though there had been a bomb inside it. "Impressive." He put the can down onto the table. "You know you're cleaning this up, right?" His gaze was playful; I knew he wasn't angry, but I also knew that he wasn't joking.

"Yeah, sorry about that. It worked though."

"I'll get the mops," said Nick, and as he walked past me, before he went through the door, he touched me reassuringly on the shoulder. When he was gone I smiled to myself triumphantly; I might be good for something after all.

CHAPTER THIRTY-TWO

Freya

The package was small, it was perfectly wrapped, and it was frightened. *Beautiful.*

My babies had captured and bound the girl expertly. I was so proud.

"Thank you, my darlings," I whispered to them, kissing each of their cheeks. "Now," I said, turning to the girl. "Let's see if we can find somewhere to put you, for the time being."

She squirmed and squeezed and cried as my babies lifted her up. She called me terrible names, actually hurting my feelings a little.

"Be careful my dear," I said to her as she was placed in her cell. "The more you struggle, the more you fear, the better you'll taste."

That shut her up.

I had more important things to worry about. Today was the day that my mentor had decided to pay me a visit, and I needed something impressive to offer for dinner.

Once the girl was quiet, curled up into a corner of the cell, I went to check on my latest protégées.

They were coming along nicely, the only screaming I could hear from them now was coming from inside their heads. They were fighting the change better than I had initially anticipated, but it wouldn't matter. I got them all, eventually.

I licked the girl's salty, teary face. She was delicious. They no longer needed chains, they stood still of their own accord. Pretty soon, they would crave their first meal. I couldn't wait. Perhaps we could save a bit of the girl for them. Perhaps.

Suddenly, my skin bristled, and I felt a tight knot of nervousness in my stomach.

He's here.

The only one to ever elicit fear from me. It was a delightful, almost sickening feeling. It reminded me that I was still alive. I just wanted to show him how well I was doing. I wanted to impress him, to still hold the title of his favourite.

I rushed to the hallway to greet him. My babies, as instructed, had already opened the door and took his coat. I stood before him in my best bright blue dress, flat shoes this time; he wouldn't approve of heels, and my hair brushed, but left to tumble over my shoulders.

"Freya."

His voice was a mere whisper, I wasn't even sure if he had opened his mouth, but I heard his voice. I hadn't seen him in almost six years, but he was a busy man, travelling the world, making sure his pupils remained up to scratch. I didn't want to disappoint.

"Sir," I said in a low voice, and bowed my head. "Please, come in."

He was taller than the last time I had seen him, or maybe it was I who was in a shorter body. He wore his usual black attire, and he took his hat off to reveal his pale, bald head. His eyes, nothing human left in them now, scrutinised my home. I'd had my babies clean everything, from the dust on the shelves to the pile of bodies cluttering up the cells. He didn't appreciate mess.

"Still imprisoned, I see," he sniffed. My heart sank immediately; I felt like a child being reprimanded.

"I'm working on it, Sir," I said, trying to sound confident rather than petulant. "Actually at this moment I am preparing..."

"Stop talking," he said, with a wave of his hand. I closed my mouth. He knelt down to meet my gaze, and cupped my face in his large hands. "My dear, I don't care about the details, I trust you. You've got out before and you'll do it again, I'm sure. I have every faith in you."

"Thank you, Sir," I replied. I had been imprisoned for far too long, I knew that, and every time I escaped, I was caught up with, and imprisoned again. But once I had the rest of my abilities, the ones that Jennifer had stolen, I would be far too powerful to keep locked up by silly magic.

My mentor could, with a mere click of his fingers, incinerate all who held me here, but, in his own words, how will his children learn if he does everything for them?

"Now," he said, straightening up and sniffing the air. "Who's for dinner?"

CHAPTER THIRTY-THREE

Aria

Over the next few days, neither of us went out of the house except to the back garden, we shifter-proofed the house with extra locks on all doors and windows, Nick showed me how the house alarm worked, he showed me the various traps he'd rigged up, and we ordered food online and had it delivered to the house.

Even though I felt safe in Laura's home, I soon became restless, and found myself pacing from room to room, unable to shake the feeling that I was just sitting around waiting for something to happen to me.

I was brought violently out of my thoughts when the telephone rang. I wondered whether to answer it or not, but then I decided it could be someone Laura knew, someone who may not be aware of what had happened. I picked up the phone and put it to my ear.

"Hello?" There was a crackling silence. "Hello?"

I waited for a few seconds, and when I still heard nothing, I put the phone down with shaking fingers. *Who could that have been? Someone who knows I'm here?*

I wrapped my cardigan tighter around me, and drew the living room curtains, even though the sun was still shining outside. I felt as though I were being watched, and in an effort to calm myself down, I put the TV on.

I decided to search the internet on Nick's laptop whilst the TV kept me company in the background. I searched for any more information on the fire at the facility, but all I could find was that there was still an ongoing investigation as to the cause. The site where it had once stood had been flattened. *That was quick.*

I then searched the words "shapeshifters" and sifted through the various web pages the search brought up. It was mostly information on folklore of humans who could turn into wolves, birds and other animals, pictures of the grotesque, painful-looking process of transmutation and stories of people in certain tribes being possessed by the souls of animals.

There was nothing to describe the shifters that had been chasing me, the ones that Nick kept in his basement. These shapeshifters had turned so seamlessly from their true form to me and back again. Could they turn into anyone they wanted to? How would I ever know if one was hiding behind someone I trusted?

I went back to the disturbing transmutation images, and almost became lost in their agony.

"You alright there?"

Nick's sudden and unexpected voice made me jump. I looked over at him.

"Yeah, sorry, just researching," I replied.

"Find anything interesting?"

"Interesting, yes. But useful? Not really."

"Okay."

I noticed then how tired he looked, how beaten down he seemed. He looked ill.

"Are you okay?" I asked.

"Yeah, I'm fine," he said.

He sat down beside me and held his head in his hands.

"Oh, yeah," I said. My sentence dripped with sarcasm. I tried to make it light, tried to make him at least smile, but it didn't work. Nick's expression panicked me; he was usually so calm, almost too much so; I hadn't seen him this shaken before.

"I just…they're going to keep coming for us, for you. I don't know if we'll be ready…"

"We'll be ready."

"But they're strong, and there must be more out there. Whoever it is, whoever is doing this, they won't stop until they have what they want."

"Well we'll train more, we'll get ready, and take them down, one by one. I'm already getting stronger every day…"

"It's not enough," Nick replied.

His eyes had become so piercing, and his jaw so set, that it was unnerving.

My cheeks flushed as he took a step towards me. "I lost you once, I can't…"

My heart was pounding, I didn't know what to do or say, or where to look. *What is he doing?*

"That won't happen again," I whispered. "We'll make sure it won't."

He was closer to me now, and I could feel the energy radiating from him, so hot, so intensely mixed up, he was as confused and conflicted as I was. I saw it all on his face, what he had gone through, what he'd lost, how this all made him capable of what he'd been doing with these shifters. He had to be tough, hard, cold, but it was a thin shell, and underneath, he was just another guy who had suffered, and who was grieving.

"We'll manage," I reassured him. "We'll train, and do more research, and we'll find whoever has been doing this, and we will destroy them. I promise."

I felt a kind of prickly heat make its way up my spine, and my hands became sweaty. Nick just nodded in agreement, he had no words at that moment. Or perhaps he did, but they were reserved for Jenny, not for me. I could see that in him too, his sorrow that I looked like her, but I wasn't, and for the first time since Nick and I had met, I desperately wanted to be everything he wanted me to be. I wanted to be Jenny, for him, and for myself, because deep down, somewhere inside, I was her. I was still her. She wasn't gone, she was just lost. I would find her, one day, I would.

I opened my arms out to Nick, and he only paused for a second before he took me and enveloped me in his warm embrace. I wrapped my arms around his waist and rested my head on his chest. I closed my eyes and heard the rhythm of his heart. He held me close and I felt him bury his face into my hair.

"I'm sorry," I whispered.

"What for?" he said softly.

"I'm sorry I can't be her for you."

I felt the rise and fall of his chest as he sighed.

"It's not your fault," he answered, his voice thick. He pulled away from me and brought my wet, flushed face up to meet his. "But don't think that makes any difference to me. I'll still protect you."

I smiled weakly at him.

"Likewise," I said.

"Sounds good then," he replied.

As he looked at me, his face suddenly clouded over, and he frowned, letting me go instantly to steady himself against the kitchen table. He groaned and rubbed his temples.

"Fuck," he said through gritted teeth. "Fucking *hell*…"

"Nick? Nick are you okay?" I asked. "What's happening? Nick?"

He crouched down onto the floor and breathed steadily. I got him a glass of water. I didn't know what else to do.

"Nick?"

He breathed deeply, sucking in air like he was drowning, and then exhaling in big puffs. *What the fuck is this?*

Then, just like that, it was over. My hand was planted firmly on my pounding heart, my eyes wide with tears.

"Are you alright?" I asked. "What was that?"

"Ah, I'm sorry Aria," he replied, getting up. "Jesus Christ…my head…"

"I got you some water," I said, feeling completely lame at that moment. He looked back at the water, and took it with shaking fingers.

"Thank you," he said. He took the glass to his mouth, and gulped it down quickly. "It was just a vision," he said.

A who? "What?"

"I have visions sometimes…it's my thing…sorry, I didn't mean to scare you."

"Oh, well I guess that's as normal as everything else that's going on," I replied.

He smiled weakly.

"What did you see?" I asked. He caught his breath before he answered my question.

"It was Mark…" he said.

"Who's Mark?"

It turned out that Mark was Nick's brother. He was five years older than Nick. He went missing when he was ten years old, and now, twenty years later, he was presumed dead. There was an investigation at the time, but nothing was found. Nick described it as Mark simply vanishing, one day, into thin air. Mark had been in his bedroom at the time, and his mother had gone in to tell him it was time for bed, and he just wasn't there anymore.

"They searched the whole house, rang the neighbours,

searched the garden, and local parks. They then called the police," Nick told me. " I don't remember much about his disappearance, but I remember the aftermath of it. My parents were never the same afterwards. They searched and searched for him, but there was no trace."

"Do you believe he's dead?" I asked. He smiled; a knowing smile that I didn't understand.

"I can't say," he replied. "If he *was* alive, he would have got in touch with us, he would be thirty years old now. But every now and again, I have a vision of him. He is either standing by my side, or in a different country somewhere, travelling, sightseeing, it's so weird."

"So he could be alive then?"

Nick shrugged his shoulders. "I always find myself in those places where I've had visions of him by my side, and he's never there. I've learned to stop expecting him now."

Nick was then silent, and I let the silence settle on us for a while.

"Sorry," he finally said. "I don't usually talk about that kind of stuff, only with…well, only with you."

I smiled bitterly. "You mean only with Jenny?"

His eyes darkened for a moment, and he managed a weak smile. He couldn't think of anything to say, because he knew I was right.

CHAPTER THIRTY-FOUR

Freya

Despite what you may think of us, we still held certain values and manners, and we dined on the young girl at the dinner table, complete with napkins and cutlery.

My babies had cut her throat, and then chopped off the bony bits, leaving only the meat left. A feast was put on for my mentor, with parts of the meat roasted, parts fried, grilled and buttered, and added to wonderful sauces made from the blood she had spilled. This was topped off with luxurious champagnes, wild fruits and fresh, warm bread.

We ate in silence; I had learnt quickly in my early days under his wing that I was only to speak when I was spoken to. My babies stood at attention, clearing plates and refilling glasses upon instruction. To create a more professional atmosphere, they had shifted into the forms of waiters and waitresses.

"These are coming along nicely, aren't they?" he commented, gesturing to my children.

I wiped my mouth with my napkin before answering.

"Yes," I replied. "I am very proud of them."

"How long do they take to transform?" he asked.

I gulped down the knot in my throat. I knew my answer wouldn't be good enough, but I couldn't lie.

"Anywhere between a few days and a week," I replied.

"A *week?!*" he cried. "That's *far* too long dear! Haven't you been practising?"

"Yes, Sir, but…"

"And I sense that a lot of your new ones have been easily killed, by humans of all things! Freya, you've become sloppy in your impatience."

I was quiet, I knew it was better to remain quiet than try to argue. He was right, anyway. So I sat, my eyes on my half eaten meal, and waited to be allowed to speak.

"The two you have strung up in there." He pointed to the cells downstairs. "How long have they been there?"

"Just…just over a week." I whispered, biting back the urge to cry.

"It's too long, Freya, too long," he said. "It's not efficient. Look, I'll show you."

He clicked his fingers at one of my children.

"You," he said. "Come here. Go out, and find me someone. Anyone. Just make it quick."

Because my babies are wholly subservient to me, it waited for my signal before moving a muscle.

"Yes. Go," I agreed, waving my hand away. Three of them left, and the others continued their waiting duties.

"My dear," he said, his voice softer. "I am merely trying to teach you. You are by far my favourite, and I just want you to fulfil your potential, that's all."

"I know, Sir."

"Good."

My babies came back soon after with a shouting, screaming man of around thirty. He was swearing, struggling, grabbing my children's hair and flesh, biting, ripping their skin. But they held him fast.

My mentor stood up.

"Now, watch," he told me, his eyes glistening with excitement.

163

He grabbed the man's head, and he immediately went limp. Before his last scream had finished echoing through the room, the transformation had begun. He grew taller, longer, his limbs stretched out, his head grew bigger, his teeth sharper, his jaw more elongated. As he opened his eyes, all that remained was the milky whiteness. He bared his long teeth, his snout twitching, and growled.

"This is as long as it should take you, Freya," my mentor said. "Maybe we need to go through techniques again."

I gazed in wonder at the shapeshifter that he had made. To my shame, it was larger than all of mine, its blue skin sharper, purer and it was a lot more powerful. *What's wrong with me?*

"In your quest to find this girl, you've lost sight of the importance of quality, Freya," he said.

"Yes, Sir. I'm sorry."

"Don't be sorry. Be better," he replied. He saw my forlorn face, and for the first time in centuries I felt like the sixteen year old I had been when I first met my mentor. His face softened.

"Anyway, enough shop talk," he said, his tone now lighter. "I've brought you some presents."

He clicked his fingers, and the shapeshifter he had so recently created, disappeared out of the passageway leading to outside, the only place I could not go. It came back a few seconds later. It handed my mentor a large box.

"Thank you," he said to the shapeshifter. I marvelled at his unwavering professionalism. "Now, this one is for your wall."

He handed me the box. I opened it excitedly. It was a head. A girl of around seventeen. She was beautiful. Her eyes had rolled up into her head, and dried blood had crusted on her upper lip, but that was nothing we couldn't fix. I could do her hair and put on a little make up before mounting her on the wall.

"Who is she?" I asked.

"You mean you don't recognise her?" He raised an eyebrow and smiled at me conspiratorially. I looked at her again. I *did* recognise her, but it was a face from so long ago, I could barely remember…

"Your first kill," he said.

"What?" I looked at the head again, and he was right. The bully, the girl I had murdered. *Oh how I cherish that memory.* But it had been a hundred and fifty years.

"How?" I asked, unable to form any other words. "How?"

"Someone owed me a favour," he replied, smiling.

I was speechless. This was such an amazing gift, and I realised then how much I didn't know about my mentor. He was so much older than me, his power was limitless, and I knew he could access worlds different to this one. I would probably never know, and probably never match, the full extent of his power.

"Thank you, Sir. Thank you so much," I replied. "This is… thank you."

He put a hand up to wave away my gratitude.

"I brought you something else," he continued. "Although maintaining perfection and high quality with your work, you must remember to also take some time out, enjoy yourself. You don't get out much, after all."

His shapeshifter disappeared again.

"That head is for your wall," he said. "And this… *this* is for your bed."

"Thank you Sir."

"You're very welcome, my child. Now, make sure this one lasts; why go for the kill when you can go for the hurt?"

"Of course, Sir."

"Until next time then, my dear. Delicious young girl, by the way."

"Thank you. Goodbye Sir."
"Goodbye Freya."

CHAPTER THIRTY-FIVE

Aria

I was sat in Laura's room on the floor. Nick told me that Jenny used to sit sometimes and attune herself to the energy, to nature, to almost become the energy itself.

I could feel Laura's back garden with beautiful flowers, the trees and fields surrounding the rows of houses, even the energies of people in the neighbouring houses. I reached my mind out and felt them all, read the different types of energies, from the oldest trees to the newest stalks, to the people next door having an argument, to the couple across the road making love. It was wonderful, being able to sense this all this around me, all this life and emotion, to not simply see it with my eyes but to know it as fact, to feel the certainty of its power. It gave me hope that perhaps not all was lost. Perhaps Nick and I would defeat the shifters, and perhaps I would get my memory back and I could be who I always should have been.

I was pulled out of my trance when heard the front door slamming open and a loud bang, followed by shouting and swearing. I got to my feet in a panic and ran downstairs. I came down to find Nick, covered in thick blue liquid, and a shifter struggling in his arms. He had a wild look in his eyes.

"Open the basement!" he shouted. "Quick!"

I said nothing in response, but followed his orders, and I opened the basement door wide and watched Nick boot the shifter down the stairs. It shrieked and crashed to the floor. Nick slammed the door shut and went to retrieve a length of rope from the kitchen.

"There were two of them," he said. "I had to kill one, but I brought this one back."

"Why?" I asked. "We already know that they want us dead, there's no way its going to give us any useful information." Nick stopped in his tracks and turned to me.

"Aria, they didn't bother to disguise themselves. They know you're here, and that scares me more than anything. The vision I had the other day, it showed me..."

"Showed you what?"

"They find us, eventually they find us."

"What? How?" *How could he have kept this from me?*

"I don't know how, and I don't know when, but I know it will be in this house. Now I'm going to get some answers out of this shifter, I need to at least try."

I marched towards him.

"Why didn't you tell me this before?" I demanded.

"I'm telling you now," he said. He then headed towards the basement, and placed his hand around the door handle. "Are you coming?"

I didn't really have a choice, this was a good a chance as any to see how my defences actually held up against them. I knew that now wasn't a good time to demand an explanation as to why he wasn't honest with me. It could wait.

Nick looked tired and angry, but I could also see that there was a part of him that was intrigued to find out what I could do. I followed him into the basement.

"Just don't get any goo on me," I replied, trying to remain confident, although my whole body shook in fear of what lay downstairs.

I stood in the basement, my heart pounding against my ribcage, a cold sweat creeping up my spine. I didn't want to be here, I wished I was anywhere else, any other place, just so I wouldn't be exposed to what I knew was about to happen.

It was more petrifying this time round though, as I knew that I was expected to join in. I didn't think I would have it in me. Even though the shifters were evil and cruel, murderous and savage, I hated seeing them tied up and helpless, with Nick beating them for information. I looked away when he hit the poor shifter in front of me, and winced when I saw the blue, florescent blood oozing from its wounds.

It was clear from the beginning that it wasn't going to speak, it just snarled at me and grinned insanely when Nick asked it anything. Its cold eyes burned into mine, it knew something that we didn't, that much was clear, but it would rather die than give us the information we needed. If it did tell us anything, perhaps the consequences of *that* would be worse than death.

"Aria," I heard Nick say. I snapped out of my thoughts, and I saw Nick looking at me expectantly. "You alright?"

"Yeah," I replied, stepping forward. "What do we do now?"

Nick stood behind the shifter, and to my horror he started untying it. I inhaled and exhaled deeply, trying to remain calm. *We can do this. There's two of us and only one of him.*

"I'll be here if you need me," Nick said.

"Okay, great," I replied. I then turned to him. "Wait, *what*?"

The excitement in Nick's eyes made me uneasy. He had grown to enjoy this.

"We're going to put practice to the test," he said in a low voice. "Don't worry, you can do this."

"But…"

My voice caught in my throat as Nick threw the rope to the

floor. He stood back, and the shifter stood up. It seemed to unfold, its limbs stretching outward as it tensed and relaxed its muscles, preparing. It towered over Nick and I, and I froze in a horrified panic. I couldn't take my eyes off its icy stare.

In a split second before it sprang towards me, I felt myself change, as my mind comprehended that it was either me or it, and it and others like it had caused me so much pain. There was no time to be afraid, or hesitant, because that could be the difference between me defeating it, and me being defeated.

I barely had time to pull the energy inside me and shoot it out through my hands. The energy flew towards the shifter, and the shifter was propelled backwards. It was only slowed down for a second before it came at me again, and I threw another shot of energy at it. It hit the shifter square in the chest, and threw it against the wall. It got up again, dazed, but still it stumbled towards me.

Choking back tears, I threw the last shot of energy, the weakest of them all, but it was enough to stop the shifter's beating heart. I felt the life drain out of it, just as at the same moment all the energy drained out of me, and I sank to the floor, exhausted.

The shifter convulsed before it broke down into a liquid mess of blue and grey ooze on the floor. It was like it had melted, become nothing. There was nothing left. I found myself sobbing, trying to catch my breath. I had killed a living thing. I knew it was evil, and that it was the only thing I could do, but I had extinguished life, and it sickened me.

Nick rushed to my side. I turned to him, looked at his smug face for a second, and then punched him in it, as hard as I could. He stumbled backwards, more from shock than from pain. *You fucking stupid, selfish bastard!*

"Get away from me," I said. I made sure I was back up the stairs and out of sight before I let myself cry.

I went back to Laura's room. I sat in her bed, the whole scenario repeating itself in my head. *What the hell does he think this is? A game?*

He could have killed me, I could have died tonight, or I could have misjudged the shot and killed Nick instead. That thought terrified me; I still didn't have full control, and to accidentally kill a human, I think it would have been the end of me.

Nick knocked on the bedroom door.

"Can I come in?" he asked.

"Fuck off," I replied, my voice barely above a whisper.

He opened the door anyway, which infuriated me. *Does he never listen?*

He left the door open and sat on the edge of the bed. I pulled the bed covers up above my shoulders, and glared at him, waiting for him to speak.

"I'm sorry," he said, but it didn't sound like an apology. It sounded like the next word he was going to say was 'but.'

"...But, we needed to know that you could do this, and I was almost certain that you could."

"*Almost* certain?" I spat. He sighed impatiently, as a person might sigh when they are trying to explain something to someone who might be stupid.

"Look, Aria, this is real life, this is what's happening, right now, to us. I know you disagree, but I needed to know that you could handle yourself." I was livid that that was all he could say to explain himself.

"What's wrong with you?" I whispered. "You could have killed us both."

I shifted down the bed and rested my head on the pillow, turning my back to him.

"I just needed to make sure," he repeated. "In case I'm ever not here."

"But I thought we were supposed to do this together," I replied.

"But I mean if something happens to me, if I can't be there…"

He meant if the shifters killed him, could I handle it alone? I turned back to him then, sitting up in the bed.

"Tell me what you saw in your vision," I said, my eyes piercing his. I demanded an answer. He looked back at me for a long time, his eyes studying my face. "Now," I seethed.

"Okay," he finally said. "The shifters came, they burst through the front door, upstairs, and they took us."

"And then what happened?"

"And then nothing, it ended there."

"Anything else? Any details that might help us?"

"No…well, Mark was part of it, trying to help us, but he won't be there."

My mind grew numb with fear. They were coming; we were sitting ducks.

"So we have to get out of here," I said. "We need to start packing, find somewhere else to stay for a while." Even as I was saying the words, I saw Nick shaking his head.

"And where would we go? They'll find us, and if we leave, we'll possibly put more people in danger."

"But we can't stay here!"

"We have to, Aria. There's nowhere else we can go. Look…" He brushed his hands through his hair. "This is why I didn't tell you."

"But we've had a warning…" I insisted, annoyed at his patronising tone.

"It wasn't a warning," Nick replied angrily. "It has to play out this way; we stay here, and see what happens. I can never change a vision, never."

His face grew dark, and in his eyes I could see he was scared. He was telling the truth. I exhaled heavily, defeated.

"So what do we do?" I asked.

"We prepare, train as much as we can, arm ourselves, protect the house. You never know, we might fight them off."

"Perhaps. Do you have any idea when this might happen?"

Nick thought for a moment.

"It was a morning, that's all I can remember. It was sunny, and I was in such a good mood…"

"Okay, so we'll get ready, and watch out for sunny mornings. Although you being in a good mood would narrow it down."

Nick chuckled, and I smiled at him. His eyes had rested upon my neck and my bare shoulders for a second, and I saw his expression become softer. He then looked away. I knew what he was thinking, but it didn't bother me. I left my shoulders as they were.

I looked at him as he studied his hands, and I had nothing to say, but at the same time I had everything to say. I wanted to tell him that even though I couldn't remember his face, or his voice or smell, I had always felt an emptiness that he had now filled.

I almost knew that he had been out there, and I knew that I could love him like how Jenny loved him. I wanted to ask him if I resembled her at all, if we shared any of the same habits, the same likes and dislikes, or if I was just a stranger now. Could he ever love me the way he loved her? I reached my hand out and took his, and he clasped his other hand tightly, almost urgently, over mine. He stayed like that for a long time. When we both grew tired, he laid down beside me, and I fell asleep with his warm, solid body next to me.

CHAPTER THIRTY-SIX

Freya

I woke up to the beautiful sight before me. She wasn't as young as I'd had previously; she was probably around twenty-five or twenty-six, but she was stunning. My mentor knew my tastes better than I knew them myself sometimes, and I was grateful to have him look out for me, and teach me. And I would be better, from now on, I wouldn't be sloppy, I would be patient. After all, all I had was time. And when I get out of this prison, I would make him even prouder.

I had spent the night enjoying myself, enjoying her, and today I felt rested, I felt relaxed and rejuvenated. My babies were closing in on Jennifer, I felt it. It wouldn't be long now. I just hoped that this time, they would succeed.

"Good morning," I said to the girl. She was naked, shivering, restrained against the bed. "How are you?"

She just looked at me with those huge, brown eyes. They were red with tears. Her mouth was taped up roughly. I took the tape off.

"My apologies," I said to her. "How are you?"

"Please, let me go," she whimpered through her tears. "Please."

"I can't do that, sweetie, sorry," I replied. "But I can get you something to eat, perhaps? Are you hungry?"

She just looked away from me, and began to cry again, huge heaving sobs that made her breasts dance before my eyes. I pushed down the urge to take pleasure in her again. I needed to make this one last. There had been instances in the past where I had been too rigorous, or too neglectful, and they'd expired before their due date. I had to take care of this one, out of fear of the consequences if nothing else.

I brought her some water and left-over bread anyway, and untied her arms before leaving her to eat, locking my bedroom door behind me. She wouldn't get out.

I went to check on Ash and Beth, and they still weren't complete. *Why is this taking so long?* They had become more than boring now, like an old toy that had lost its novelty. The sooner they were turned, the better, then I could send them out personally to fetch Jennifer for me. It would be ironic. But for now they offered no form of entertainment for me, and I found myself growing even more bored.

This was dangerous, because when I grew bored, I grew ratty, and nothing that is then subsequently brought to me gives me any pleasure. I could go back into my bedroom and play with my new girl a bit more, but after that, what? What else is there?

I glided aimlessly through the rooms of my house, my prison. The cells were still clean, and the bones of the girl we had eaten had been disposed of. The scraps had been given to my children, and they fought over the meat, scratching and biting at each other for the last piece. It was barbaric. It made me proud.

I ended up in the dining room, and just beyond that was the front door. It was a daily reminder, a daily tease, that I couldn't cross it. Of course I had tried, but magics had held me back. But every now and again I liked to test it, to push its boundaries, and see how far I got.

I touched the smooth handle, arrogant in its thickness, the door grainy and old.

I opened the door in one swift movement. That was the easy

part. Beyond it was a tunnel, that led up and up, and eventually to outside. I could smell the fresh air, feel the light against my skin. It almost brought tears to my eyes. I took a step forward. It was like moving through tar, everything felt heavy. I took another step. That was when the pain kicked in.

My skin, my very soul, was burning. I took another step, and the burning increased. In my darkest days, when I was at my lowest, this was the place where I would battle with my own death, knowing that, if I got through the pain, if I took the steps, at the other end I would cease to exist, and all this would be over. But the pain always won. I guess I was a coward.

I felt now like sandpaper was stripping away my skin, like it was being sizzled under a hot flame. I felt sick. *No, come on. You can go further.* The heat was immense. I didn't want to spoil this beautiful body, but I couldn't let it win again. It beat me every time. Another step, and I was sick all down my dress. Another one, and my skin began to peel away from my flesh. *Okay, stop now, you've had your fun. It's not worth it, not when you're so close.*

I crawled back down the hallway, and closed the door. I checked my body. Parts of my hair had fallen out, and my skin had almost completely burnt away. But it was nothing I couldn't fix. Unless…unless I swapped.

Yes, that's what I'll do, I'll swap.

CHAPTER THIRTY-SEVEN

Aria

I woke up the next day and Nick had gone. I ran to the window in a panic, and threw open the curtains. It was raining.

I sighed in relief, and then went to put some clothes on and see where he had gone. I found some jeans and a plain green t-shirt. I left the bedroom and stood at the top of the landing.

That was where I froze on the spot, my heart in my mouth. I heard voices drifting up from downstairs. I tried to hear what they were saying, but the voices were muffled, as though they were whispering. I looked around upstairs for Nick. He wasn't there.

Dread filled my mind as I crept down the stairs. What if there was a shifter downstairs, and it had captured him? What if there were two downstairs, and Nick wasn't here at all? What if they'd already killed him and they were whispering about what to do with me?

I searched for something to arm myself with, and I found a large umbrella by the front door. It was pointed at the end with a sturdy metal.

I listened for the voices, and when I was certain that I knew where they were, I made my way to the kitchen. I eased open the door, the umbrella pointy-end first poised above my head. My eyes fell on Nick, sitting at the kitchen table, a slice of toast in his hand. He was laughing with a young girl who was stood at the sink. She had her back to me, and she was doing the washing up.

Nick's smile instantly faded as he turned to see me, ready to strike, and he mouthed "*No!*" at me and gestured wildly with his hands. The young girl turned to him and he resumed his normal stance, and she smiled and then turned to me.

I had just enough time to bring the umbrella down from over my head and put it behind the door. The young girl made a small, squeaking sound upon seeing me and she dried her hands on a tea-towel. She then fixed her hair and stepped towards me, a wide smile spreading over her face.

"Hello, Aria," she said in a low voice.

"Hello," I replied. She had long, dark hair and a small nose, with big brown eyes and small lips. She wore faded blue jeans and a pink jumper. She looked about fifteen or sixteen years of age. She held out her hand, and I took it.

"It's nice to meet you, I'm Kara, Kara Matthews."

"Nice to meet you. Are you a friend of Nick's?"

"Yes," she replied. "But I'm also a friend of yours."

I looked at her blankly, I had never met this girl before, and my heart sank when I realised that she must have been a friend of Jenny's.

"I'm sorry, I…" I began, but she waved her hand to quieten me. I closed my mouth.

"Nick told me about what happened to you, it must be dreadful," she said. In her eyes I could see a glimmer of pain as she looked at me; she had suffered, she had lost, and she was so young. All I could do was nod.

"Come and sit down," Nick said to me, and he pulled out the other stool for me to sit in. I sat down heavily.

"I had to come and see you," Kara said. "When Nick told me you had been found, I just needed to see for myself, and here you are." She smiled at me, but tears stung her eyes. "You helped me in so many ways, more ways than I thought possible."

"Did we know each other at the facility?" I asked. Her intensity was a little too much for me so early in the morning, especially as I had no idea who she was. Her face became red and she put a hand to her mouth as tears fell down her cheeks.

"Yes," I heard her whisper. Nick stood up and gave her some tissue so she could wipe her eyes. "I'm sorry," she said to me. "I didn't want to do it like this."

Nick told her to take his seat, and so she sat, trying to compose herself.

"Kara has abilities like us," he said to me. "She came to the facility for help, and she was assigned to you."

"I remember when we first met," Kara said, her voice thick. "I was so scared and confused, and you took me to your office, and you gave me a plant." She laughed then. "I remember wondering what the hell you were doing, as the plant was nearly dead. You sat down in front of me, and closed your eyes. The plant suddenly bloomed into life, it was so amazing. You told me…"

She paused for a second and held the tissue to her face. Her breath came out short, racked, and I instinctively took her other hand in mine, and squeezed it. She squeezed back. She began again.

"You told me that I was safe here, and I was accepted, and that you would help me. You made me feel normal when everyone else I knew called me a freak or a liar. You saved me, Aria."

She blew her nose, and wiped her eyes.

"And you let me keep the plant."

She then chuckled, and I smiled. A lump had formed in my throat, and in that moment I hated, more than I had ever hated it up until that moment, that I couldn't remember. I didn't feel worthy of the praise she was giving me. I didn't deserve her kind words. I bit my lip as it trembled.

"It wasn't me," I said weakly.

Kara looked up at me, her eyes wide.

"Yes, it was. Even if you can't remember it now, it was you, and if you remember nothing else, remember that you did help people, kids like me, and we are so grateful to you." I looked at her through blurry eyes, and she put her arms around me. We hugged tightly, fiercely.

"I still have nightmares about what happened that day," she said, her voice muffled by my shoulder. "If Nick hadn't got us out when he did…"

"I wish I could have nightmares about what happened," I replied.

We parted, and she wiped her face one last time. She then brushed back her hair with her fingers.

"Well, I should go," Kara said, her words coming out in a sigh. "I'll be late for college."

"Okay," I replied. "It was really good to meet you."

"It was great to meet you, Aria."

"Come back anytime, won't you?" I asked.

Her sad, grateful smile almost broke my heart.

"Definitely," she replied. "Bye," She turned to Nick. "Bye, Nick."

"Bye Kara," he said. I then watched as she pulled her backpack onto her shoulders, and left by the front door, clicking it into place. I sighed heavily and turned back to Nick.

"How much does she know?" I asked him. He'd been drying a few pots that Kara had just washed, and he was so intently concentrated on this task, I wasn't sure if he'd heard me at first.

But then I saw his face.

"Are you okay?" I asked, stepping towards him. He put a plate down onto the worktop, and leaned against it, the tea-towel in his other hand.

"Yeah, yes, I'm fine. She doesn't know much, just that there was a fire, people died. I got her out before a lot of the trouble began. But its been difficult, for everyone."

"Did she know Laura?"

"Yeah," Nick replied. "She'd made friends with some other kids there too, kids whose deaths she had to deal with. But, she's strong, she can cope with it, and that's because of you."

"But I don't remember her, I don't remember doing any of these things you're congratulating me on doing," I replied. I was growing angry, not at them, but at my stupid self. I was so useless I couldn't even remember the people around me who loved me.

"It doesn't matter, we'll get your memory back one day, I promise."

"Its not just about that," I said. I hated that I couldn't keep the anger out of my voice. "I don't deserve any of this. I have done nothing to justify this love from people, the only thing I'm good at is putting them in danger. Until I get my memory back, am I to forever walk around meeting people who think so highly of me for reasons I can't understand? People who I have supposedly helped, changed their lives, and am I to forever apologise and tell them that I don't recall ever meeting them before? What if its already happened? What if someone in the street has already come across me, and waved, or said hello, and I haven't even given them a second glance? What do I do in that situation?"

I took a deep breath, shocked at the words that had come pouring out of my mouth. I clamped my mouth shut, afraid of what else I might say. Nick looked at me, astounded.

"I don't know, Aria," he replied. "I don't know what you would do in those situations, but if it were me, I would just be grateful that there were such people out there.

"So you think I'm ungrateful?"

"No, you know that's not what I meant…"

"Isn't it?"

"Of course not. Look, we'll just get through this together, each day as it comes. We'll train, and we'll destroy those bastards, and we'll get your memory back, somehow, we will."

I covered my face in my hands, defeated.

"I just don't know what to do with myself," I sobbed. It was so unfair.

When Ash and Beth were here, I could almost forget, and I would have been happy spending the rest of my life with them. But now they were gone, they probably never existed in the first place, and my past kept coming back to greet me, to thank me for what I had done, who I used to be, and I felt as though I was being mocked by it. Who would render me so helpless like this? Who hated me that much as to take everything away from me?

"It's alright," Nick whispered, and I felt him stand behind me. He put a hand on my shoulder. A few minutes passed before I was able to speak again.

"So what abilities does Kara have?" I asked.

"She can talk to people when normally they can't communicate," he replied.

I wiped my eyes and Nick sat beside me.

"What does that mean?"

"Say, for example, someone is dying, or delirious, or they find themselves in a situation in which they can't speak, Kara can communicate with them. She can hear their voice, clear as day. It first happened with her Grandmother, when she lay dying. Everyone else heard the muddled, incoherent words of someone whose brain is shutting down but Kara could hear what her Grandmother actually wanted to say."

"That's extraordinary," I said, amazed. "That's such a wonderful gift to possess."

"Yes, but it was scary," Nick replied. "And her parents wouldn't believe her when she told them. They actually became quite angry, and that's why they brought her to us, to have us 'fix' her." He chuckled. "I've come across so many ignorant parents. But anyway, you helped her to overcome her fear of what she could do, and now she's at college. She wants to make something of her life."

"I'm glad," I said. I couldn't believe how much Kara had had to deal with, and how strong she had become. She was younger than me, but she was so inspiring.

"And whether you like it or not," Nick continued. "That courage, and acceptance of herself, is at least in part down to you."

We looked at each other for a long time, speaking without words. I needed to know what I was to him; was I just Aria, a friend who he was helping, or was I, could I ever be, the person he wanted most in the whole world? He was hesitant, I understood that, but I sat, waiting for him to make his decision.

He then leaned in so close to me, and our lips met, lightly, nervously, only for a second, but it was like electricity started coursing through my veins. I became faint from the high that it gave me; in some ways it was stronger than the energy.

Nick then kissed me more firmly, and I felt my face grow hot. He then kissed my cheeks, my neck, and I found myself sighing deeply, letting him pull me closer. My head emptied of all thoughts, all worries, and it left me with just the desire to be with him.

He took me into his arms again, and we made our way up the stairs into his bedroom. We kissed as he peeled off my clothes, and touched me as though he'd done it a thousand times. *He has done this a thousand times, he knows you better than you know yourself.*

We continued to kiss, and he touched my trembling skin lightly with his fingertips. I wanted to be everything he wished I was.

He slowly slid his fingers underneath the waistband of my underwear, and I moaned softly as I felt him push my flesh apart. I was aching now, and although I was nervous, I wanted this to happen, so much.

When he entered me, I gasped, feeling the pain only for a few seconds, before it gave way to something else. My whole body trembled, tingled. Nick held me tightly, his arms enveloping me close to his warm, solid body.

"I love you," he whispered, "I love you so much."

I kept silent, not knowing what to say back.

CHAPTER THIRTY-EIGHT

Freya

My old body looked disgusting. Hideous. Her skin had peeled away, revealing blackened flesh under it, she was mostly bald. Her breath came out in short, sharp bursts and her scalded eyes darted around the room. But she wasn't frightened, in pain yes, but frightened...I peered closer...no, not even a little bit. She was relieved. Relieved to be free.

She looked at me, in my new body, and whispered something I couldn't quite hear.

I bent down closer.

"I'm sorry," she whispered. "I'm sorry."

"You're sorry?" I asked, confused. "Sorry for what?"

"For what I did...to you," she breathed.

I looked at her burnt face.

"You didn't do anything to me, sweetheart," I said. I felt my new body, her skin, her slightly larger breasts, bigger thighs, arms. She tasted even sweeter on the inside.

"I'm not talking to you, you bitch." As she said this to me, blood flew out of her mouth and splattered over her chin. She was talking to the girl inside my new body. The one I had spent the night with.

"She can't hear you," I chided, smiling.

"Yes, she can," she replied. "She can."

"Well, go on then, what are you sorry for?"

"For what I did...to you...to others...I deserve this."

"Well, you're right about that," I said. "And how do you know she didn't enjoy what you did?"

She just glared at me, her scarred face bent into a frown. Smoke was still coming off her skin.

I then pulled out a knife from my bedside drawer. I held it against her throat.

"Any last words?" I asked.

I slit her throat before she had a chance to respond. She bled out, and died. But, as I've said before, she died with a smile on her face.

Turning around to face my bedroom door, I knew what was coming before my children had a chance to tell me.

Jennifer, she had been found.

And she was on her way.

CHAPTER THIRTY-NINE

Aria

I woke up with a sigh of contentment a few hours later, stretching my arms out in front of me. I looked over at Nick, who was still sleeping peacefully, a strange half smile on his lips. His hair stuck out at all angles, and his eyes moved rapidly under his eyelids; he must have been dreaming. I sat up in bed, and decided to have a bath.

Pulling on my dressing gown, I made my way to the bathroom. I felt happier than I had felt in weeks, I was buzzing with excitement.

As I turned on the bath taps and secured the plug, I thought about the day I would get my memory back. After last night it was no longer a possibility, but a certainty to me; there was no other alternative. I needed my memory and I would do anything to get it back, and I would then remember everything we used to have; all the places we visited, the things we had done together, promised each other. Then when I see photos of our past, I can think fondly on them instead of wondering who people were and trying desperately to connect with the girl who looked like me, but wasn't.

I climbed into the hot, rising water, leaned back, and closed my eyes. I sank my head underneath, and I lay for a few seconds, tranquil, unmoving, as though time had stopped. I came back up, sucked in the fresh, damp air, and ran my fingers through my wet hair.

But something more imminent needed to be dealt with first. I needed to focus my time on building up my strength, with Nick's help, and find out exactly what they wanted with me.

Then when I finally get my memory back, when those memories of my loved ones came crashing back to me, I would remember that I'd done all I could to extinguish the evil that had killed them all. I opened my eyes and started when I saw Nick standing over me, surprised that I hadn't heard him come in.

"You scared me," I laughed. He smiled at me.

"Sorry, I didn't mean to," he replied. I saw that he had dressed already, and looked down to notice he'd put his shoes on.

"Where are you going?" I asked him. He just kept smiling at me, unmoving, not saying a word. His face was strangely blank, and his eyes were unusually intense, almost burning into my own. The smile on his face turned into a sickly looking smirk, as his eyes then drifted up and down my body. Something wasn't right. I sat up.

"Are you okay?" I asked, folding my arms across my chest.

His eyes flashed back towards my face, and the ugly smirk became a grimace, and he reached out his hand and wrapped it around my throat. I felt a huge force push me down under the water, and I cracked the back of my head on the bathtub. Flailing my arms and legs, and screaming under the water, I tried in vain to find something to hold on to, and pull myself up with. Panic overwhelmed me, and my lungs felt as though they would burst. I inhaled a mouthful of bath-water, and I struggled to maintain consciousness. *Oh my God, this is it; I'm going to die.*

I had admitted defeat when I felt two arms wrap around me and pull me out the water. I was pulled out of the bath and on to the floor, and then I was shaken violently.

I heard Nick's voice, but it was so muffled, far away. I couldn't make out what he was saying. After a few seconds I rushed back to myself, to the moment, to reality, and I started coughing so hard, I couldn't breathe. Water and bile came rushing out of my mouth, out of my lungs, and I felt Nick's hand come down hard on my back, over and over.

I then sucked in the wonderful, dewy air around me, filling my lungs with it, my full focus returning after a few moments. I opened my eyes to find Nick holding me, he was shaking and sweaty, his face red and blotched. He looked at me in relief, then held me close to him. He was still in his underwear, unshaven, his hair a knotted mess. I laid there for a few seconds, letting him stroke my hair and kiss my face, before I asked what the hell happened.

"It...just appeared...I heard splashing and...it was just here..." Nick said, breathless.

I looked around and I noticed a kitchen knife, bloody with blue goo, on the floor. Next to it was the sodden mess of the remains of the shifter. *How did it get in without us noticing?* I looked back at Nick.

"What's our plan of action then?" I said, standing up shakily. But he wasn't listening to me, he was somewhere else. His face was pale, and his hands were trembling.

"Nick? Come on, we need to get ready. Nick?" The fear in his eyes scared me to death; he knew this was it, this was what his vision had shown him, today is the day it happens. I tried to pull him up from the bathroom floor.

"Nick!"

He then turned to me, as if snapping out of a stupor or a daydream, and jumped up. He ran to the hallway just outside the bathroom, and flung open the curtains. The sun shone down, lighting everything up in its beautiful glow. I began to tremble with fright.

"This is it," he said. "Shit." He ran back to me and grabbed my arm. "They will be back, there will be more, I don't know how long we've got."

"Okay," I replied, trying to remain calm. "What do we do?" He looked at me.

"First thing's first, put some clothes on. I'll take a look around, and see if any more have arrived."

"Right."

Nick made his way downstairs, and I steadily started making my way back to the bedroom. I quickly pulled on some jeans and a top, cursing my shaking hands. On the first floor of Laura's house, I wasn't sure if I could collect any energy, I had to be lower to the earth. I decided to follow Nick downstairs, but I hadn't got very far when I heard the door burst open. Nick yelled over to me, and blood started pumping hard in my ears. I froze in terror.

"Run! Run, Aria! RUN!"

They are here, they've come to take me.

Nick's voice filled me with terror. Shifters had come to the house before, but this was different. There were more of them, and they knew for certain that I was here. *They take us, Nick's so terrified because he knows they take us. Did he tell me everything?*

His last yell was cut short by a loud thump, and I heard a sound like a large bag of sand falling to the floor. I looked around, but there was nowhere I could run, nobody I could call out to. There were at least half a dozen of them, and I wasn't nearly strong enough to pull energy from where I was. They glided up the stairs, straight for me.

The first shifter to make its way to the landing darted towards me, and I braced myself for impact. But it suddenly stopped, and appeared to leap sideways, straight into the wall. It looked around, dazed, and the others stopped momentarily. The second shifter fell backwards onto the first, and I watched as they looked around, puzzled.

The first one got up again, and I took a step back as it fixed its eyes back on me, and glided to where I was stood. I heard a loud thump, and the shifter was knocked off its feet by something I couldn't see. It was out cold.

I tried to make a run for it, down the stairs and out the door, but there were too many of them. The last thing I remember before they took me was the sound of laughter. A woman's laughter, drowning out everything else around me. It was deafening.

* * *

I woke up with a jump, and immediately felt pain rush through my body. I was stiff, and I ached.

Looking around, I saw that I was in a cell, there were bars on one side, and brick all around the other sides. It was approximately three metres wide and about a metre deep. I fought back the claustrophobia building inside me. I looked beyond the cell bars, and there was only a hallway, and other cells, which were empty. Candles flickered on the damp, old walls.

I strained my neck to see if Nick was around, but I couldn't see or hear him. Holding the bars tightly in my hands, I tried to push open the cell door. It was locked. A lonely, empty feeling crept up inside me, and I urgently tried to reach out, to find energy from anyone, anything, nearby, but there was nothing. This place was...dead. All around, there was nothing; no happiness, no hope, it was filled with despair.

My heart started pounding as heard I somebody coming. A shifter. I heard its jaws snapping and its large hands and feet pounded against the wet, stone slabs.

"What do you want?" I said, my voice high and shrill with panic.

It ignored my question, and proceeded to open the lock on my door, using its elongated, pasty arms to swing the door open without getting too close to me. It then stood, waiting patiently, almost vacantly, for me to step through. So I did, and it locked the cell back up behind me.

It then crawled to the exit in front of me, and gestured for me to follow. I paused for a second, not knowing what to do, looking around for another exit, but there was nothing. No windows, no other hallways or doors, just a small room with a set of empty cells. I turned back around to see the shifter looking at me. It chuckled as if it knew what I was searching for, and that it knew all along that my efforts were in vain. I had no choice but to follow it.

The corridor was narrow and it smelt musty and old, and it seemed to stretch on forever. The shifter suddenly veered off towards the right. I followed, and soon I was presented with a large room, once again filled with nothing except a few empty cells.

Wait, there is something. A movement, a figure.

I stopped dead in my tracks. There were in fact two figures, sitting side by side at the back of one of the cells. I peered closer, and saw two pairs of pale, lifeless eyes. My eyes took a few seconds to adjust to the level of darkness, and once they did, I saw the two figures clearly.

One was a young guy, around nineteen, his sandy hair clinging to his perspiring, expressionless face. The other figure was a long-haired girl, very slight, with mousy features. *No! My God is this real?*

Running forward in a rushed panic, I held my hands out to

touch them. I searched their creamy eyes for some sort of recognition or reaction, but there was none. They seemed to not notice I was here, I doubted they knew where they were or what was happening.

"I promise," I seethed as the shifter grabbed my arm to take me away, "I promise I will get you out, both of you. Just hold on, please."

I had just enough time to lightly touch Beth's dirty, bloody hand, before the shifter dragged me away.

CHAPTER FORTY

Aria

I was still kicking and screaming when the shifter dropped me from his powerful shoulders hard onto the floor. My right knee smacked against the concrete, and I winced in pain.

I looked up to see a room, filled with light and colour, a room so very different from the cells down the corridors. It felt like I was in a different place; there were beautiful paintings hanging from the rose pink walls, extravagant trinkets and ornaments, a glass table, a grand wardrobe, a few dusty sets of drawers, and stacks upon stacks of books.

There was a whole side of the wall dedicated to them, there must have been about twelve book shelf units, all full to the brim. And just above that…heads. A row of severed heads. I held my hand to my mouth, fighting back nausea. There was a large, wooden door at the other end. I was contemplating whether this could be a possible escape route when the door opened, and from out of it came five more shifters, tall, frightening, with the same lifeless eyes and expressionless faces.

I stood up, ready for a confrontation, biting back the terror rising inside me. They crawled along silently, the light reflecting off their bald heads and shiny, translucent skin. But then they stopped, in a line, facing me. I stood for a second, confused, until I saw someone else step out from the doorway and into the room. It was a woman; she was tall, beautiful, with pale skin and dark hair. She looked almost porcelain. She wore a long, white dress that rippled as she moved. Her hips swayed rhythmically, and her large, blue eyes flashed at me in delight. Only she wasn't as she seemed; there was something wrong, something hopeless and empty about her. Accompanying this stunning woman was a dark, overpowering surge of what I could only describe as evil, emanating from every pore of her being, and I instinctively took a step back. But there was no way out, no way I could escape her. She smiled at me in amusement, and stopped inches away from my face. I stood still, my heart pounding, as she closed her eyes and inhaled, taking in my scent. She then exhaled slowly in satisfaction, and opened her eyes again. They pierced my own.

"Finally," she said, reaching out and stroking my face with her soft, delicate hand. "My name is Freya."

She spoke in a low whisper, like the sound of trees blowing in the wind. Her mouth opened, and she licked her top lip, as if wondering how to proceed. "I believe you have something that belongs to me."

"What?"

I felt a rage inside the pit of my stomach that made my whole body itch. How dare she send her servants to bring me to this horrible place?

She continued to look at me with those sharp, greedy eyes and waited for my response. I stood there in silence, wondering what it was that I could possibly have that belonged to her. But then, I felt my blood run cold with the realization; I knew what she meant. But there was no way she was ever going to take it from me.

"I don't have anything that belongs to you," I seethed, willing myself to keep my arms at my sides and not grab her by the throat. Her eyes flashed; she was enjoying the challenge.

"I think you do," she breathed, her words raspy, almost

disappearing into the thin, stale air. I ground down my teeth and clenched my fists. *You won't break me, you can try, but you won't break me.* She sighed, hard, and brought her slender hands to rest on her round hips.

"Sit down," she gestured to me, pointing over to a brown, leather sofa with a bright, golden throw rug draped over it.

"I'll stand, thank you," I replied, not moving a muscle.

She then grabbed my shoulders hard, and I felt the sharp sting of her palm across my face before I even saw her raise it.

"I said SIT DOWN!" she yelled, and so I sat down unsteadily, pain shooting across my cheek into my eye socket.

She glided into the space next to me on the sofa, her gold bracelets jangling with her movements. She was all dressed up with nowhere to go.

"Now, there's no need for this to get ugly," she whispered, and glanced across the room, where to my shock the shifters had silently formed a circle around us. I was trapped.

"What do you want from me?" I asked, my resolve gone, my hands trembling in my lap. She smiled, a sickly, selfish sort of smile, her white teeth showing through only a little.

"I want to propose a trade."

Suddenly, out of nowhere, Nick came stumbling into the room. He was followed by more shifters, pushing him forwards. His eyes were wild, and beads of sweat stuck to his face. His eyes then landed on mine, he tried to make his way over to me, but he didn't get very far before he was stopped by a large, elongated hand on his shoulder. He stared at Freya in bewilderment, his nostrils flaring as he sucked in the air around him. He was breathless with anger.

"Let her go, now!" he shouted at her, but that just made the shifters hold him harder, their hands grasping his body and squeezing until he was still. Freya chuckled, unimpressed with his efforts. She turned back to me.

"Works of art aren't they?" she asked me, gesturing to the empty cases masquerading as humans. "My workforce."

"They are an abomination," I replied. "Evil, like you."

"Not quite true you see. They didn't start out this way. They were all human, once upon a time," she replied, looking over at them wistfully.

My heart ached with guilt; all those shifters that Nick had brought back to the house, all the ones he had tied up and tortured, and then killed, all of them were once human. The one I killed was once human. They really were doing all this against their will. Guilt swept over me, how could I have done this? I should have helped them.

"But…How?" I asked, my voice small.

"That's not really why I brought you here, sweetie, maybe we can talk afterwards," she smiled.

I peered over at their unblinking, un-emotive eyes, their gaunt faces, their long, strong arms. They towered above Nick, overwhelming in their presence, but I could not detect any human part left in them. They were husks. It didn't make me feel better though. But why did she need them? She seemed powerful enough herself to get anything she wanted from outside.

"You're trapped here, aren't you?" I said, looking around and seeing the large room for what it actually was. All her belongings were in here, everything she owned. There were no windows, there was no light, only doors to the caves down below. It was a prison, it was her prison. She looked back at me in surprise at first, and then in mock admiration.

"Why, aren't you observant?" she chided. "Well done."

"You must have done something terrible."

"That was a long time ago," she whispered. "Too long for me to count the decades anymore. The point is, anyway, that I am here, asking you for a trade. So, are you going to listen?"

My curiosity gave way, and I nodded in confirmation.

"Good," she said, and sat back deeper into the sofa. "I can give you back your memory. All I need is the energy, that's all." Her eyes shone in excitement, and I froze at her words.

"You took my memory from me?" My voice came out feeble, childish, but I needed to know, I needed to know for sure. She laughed at me then, a high, shrill cackle.

"Not me, I'm afraid. Genius, though."

"You're lying," I spat.

"No, I'm not." She leaned in closer to me. She was too close, I felt repulsed by the fact that I was sitting next to her.

"Get away from me!" I screamed, backing away. "You killed all my friends! My family! Why? Why did you have to kill everyone, if you just wanted me?!"

I brought my hands up to my face and let out a sob, anger shaking me inside so hard that I felt light-headed. I slumped to the floor, landing on my knees, unable to support myself any longer. There was a long silence before I realized that my raspy breaths were the only sound in the room.

"For God's sake!" she yelled. "You're just embarrassing yourself now. I don't owe you any answers, you're just a human. After this is over, I think I'll eat you. Now, sit still."

She grabbed my head, and I felt her squeezing it so hard I could feel my blood pumping hard in my temples. *What is she doing?* Nick saw what was happening and tried to free himself from the shifter's grasp.

"You need to be whole, for me to then carve out of you what's mine," she whispered into my ear. I tried to bat her arms away, but she was too strong, and I felt myself losing consciousness.

Everything went black. The last thing I heard was Nick, screaming my name.

CHAPTER FORTY-ONE
FRIDAY, 20TH JULY 2007

Jenny

"Laura, please! The whole place is burning, we have to get out of here!"

"Right," she replied, hurrying towards me. "We need to find somewhere safe until we know for sure those things aren't outside waiting for us."

She grabbed my arm and led me down the corridor. All I could think about was Nick; I wondered if he was still alive. They had taken over so fast, slaughtered so many people so quickly…I couldn't bear to think about it.

"Laura, what's going on? Please, you have to tell me!"

She ignored my question.

"I know! The supply room! It has a huge lock on its door, they won't be able to get in there," she said to me, her red eyes glistening with tears. "Let's go!"

She pulled me down another corridor, where several bodies blocked the passageway, some of them were children, my children. Their faces were dirty with blood, their eyes open, fixed in that state of shock.

I sobbed into Laura's shoulder as she pulled me towards her, and we carried on down the hall. We ran down a flight of stairs onto the ground floor, and turned a corner. Laura then took out her keys and opened the door. She stepped into the room, pulling me inside with her. I felt a wave of hysteria hit me.

"Laura! Please! What's happening?" I cried.

Laura closed the large metal door behind us, and we sat on the dirty floor, breathing heavily in the darkness. She grabbed me and clung onto me tight, stroking my blood-matted hair. Pain shot through my body, it was overwhelming. My eyes hurt, and my head spun.

"I'm so sorry," she said. "I didn't mean for any of this."

"This? What? Tell me what's going on!"

"I have seen these creatures before," she said to me.

I sat with my hand enveloped tightly in hers. She was shaking.

"Where?"

"In our house, my darling. They came after you when you were little."

"*What? Why?*" I asked, my voice high with panic.

Laura sighed. "I don't know, sweetie. Please try and stay quiet."

"Why didn't you tell me?" I asked. "They could have come back at any point!"

"Don't you think I know that?" she whispered through her teeth. "We had security set up for years afterwards, but they never came again. I…thought it was over. I hoped…"

"So," I whispered, my voice shaking. "So…it was me, I did this…"

"No, sweetheart…"

"Laura, I killed everybody! I killed the children!"

"No, Jenny, you didn't. Those monsters outside did, you have to remember that."

I had to make this right; I had to hand myself in to them, so they could stop all this. I stood up and rushed to the door.

"Where are you going?" Laura whispered, grabbing my arm and pulling me back down to the ground.

201

"I'll just give them what they want, then everything will be okay again."

"No! Don't you understand? They will kill you! We need to stay here. We've hidden you for all these years, there is no way they are getting their hands on you now!"

Laura sat back on the dirty floor, and put her head in her hands. "What a mess…" she said through her tears. I sat with her, and we held each other tightly.

How could I live with myself knowing all this was my fault? I couldn't, I knew that. Children who came to us for help, who I had bonded with, were dead. My best friend in the whole world was missing; I would probably never see him again. *Nick, if only I had told you how much you mean to me.*

"You have to take it away," I whispered to Laura as we sat in the dark, listening for any more movement outside.

"What?" she asked.

"You have to take it away, what you just told me. I can't…I won't be able to live with myself. Laura, please."

"I'm not even going to consider doing what you're asking me to do! I don't use my abilities for that. Jenny, it was *not* your fault, you have to believe me. If anyone has to be blamed it should be myself, I should have acted more quickly, been more prepared."

I shook my head, I was hysterical, and I could feel it rising up from inside me. I didn't want to know this; I couldn't live with this knowledge.

"Laura, please, just take it away. You can tell me anything; say that we've had to move away for some reason. Tell me anything, please, just not this! Not this!"

I grabbed at my hair, pulling it out. I couldn't handle this, I wasn't strong, I was weak and I hated myself for it. I didn't know

I could be so feeble. Laura paused, and then gently put her hands on mine and pulled them from my tangled hair.

"Okay," she said. "Okay, I'll take it out, and I'll have to find something to tell you in its place. But just so you know the severity of what you are asking me, do not blame me if you ever find out about this."

"I won't! I promise!" I said. I felt ashamed at my cowardice, but I knew that this would crush me, completely, I knew that I couldn't carry on knowing what I had caused.

"Right, stay still," she said. I closed my eyes and waited as she held my face between her hands. I felt a tingle, something worming its way inside. She then let go.

"Okay, it will take a few minutes. I'm going to go and find other survivors and bring them back here. By then, you'll have forgotten what I just told you. I'll think of what to tell you instead."

I thought for a second, I didn't want to be left here alone, but there might be other survivors out there. *God please let there be other survivors.*

"Okay," I said.

"I love you Jenny."

"I love you too." I tried to relax, I tried to ignore the screaming outside the door.

I watched as Laura opened the front door again carefully. I wanted desperately to go with her, but I would be useless at this point.

We hadn't realised that the creature had been waiting just outside the door. It grabbed Laura, and punched straight through her chest. She screamed, and then the scream turned into a gurgle, and she was dead before she hit the floor.

"No!" I yelled. I rushed over to her. "Oh God! No! Please!"

The creature was trying to get into the room, and somehow I managed to push it back and lock the door again. I grabbed Laura and pulled her to the back of the room. I knew she was dead, I knew that, but I held her anyway, and wept.

The feeling inside my head was still there, and I stopped crying as I realised that now Laura was dead, there was no one to stop the process. Instead of erasing what I had just been told, it would erase everything. I was dead.

I heard more creatures outside. I pulled myself to the middle of the room, and gritted my teeth.

I'm Jenny...I'm Jenny...For God's sake this is madness...you know who you are...come on you bastards I'll fucking kill all of you...I'm Jenny...I...

CHAPTER FORTY-TWO

Jenny

The fog in my mind cleared, my memories returned from the dark depths of the amnesia that had confused me for so long. I closed my eyes as the faces of my loved ones danced around in the darkness, laughing, crying, and smiling at me. I remembered it all: my ability, everything I had been taught, my whole life at the facility, in Laura's beautiful house, where it was just the two of us against the world. I remembered making love to Nick, our ups and downs, our arguments, our reconciliations.

I remembered Kara, and I was mortified at the way I had behaved in front of her. I remembered the other children, the joy I felt when they made progress during our sessions. I remembered their idiotic parents pleading with us to fix them. I remembered Carl, the wisest person I had ever met, the person who I respected the most.

I finally remembered that girl in the pictures, the girl who enjoyed life and worked hard improving the lives of those gifted children. Laura, her bright, excited eyes, her unwavering energy and spirit. I remembered looking at her corpse, and looking at it without recognition, in bewilderment rather than sorrow. I would have held her cold body to mine, and wept. She would have done anything for me, including the last thing I ever asked her do to.

My whole life flashed in front of my eyes, and it felt like I was dying. Sinking to the ground with a heavy sigh, I cried out in anger and frustration, my body weak and limp.

I gagged, and tried to overcome the wave of nausea. I brought my hands up to my face and wept.

How can I live with myself? What have I done? Why didn't she tell me?

They had all lied to me and Nick; my own family had kept something this important from me. I felt so betrayed.

"Your fault," I heard Freya say, her voice a whisper. "Your mess. You killed all those people. You should have handed yourself in to us, and you would have saved everyone." She then laughed. "How tragic would it have been if she had erased everything, making you as helpless as a new-born."

Her fingers delicately stroked my hair, and I shrank away from it.

"Fuck you," I mumbled.

I then noticed Nick, who had been struggling with the shifters to let him free, and had subsequently received a burst lip for his trouble.

"What is she talking about?" he asked me. *What must he think of me now?*

After months of searching, loneliness and pain, I found what I was looking for, and immediately wanted to give it back.

"Jenny?" Nick uttered, still held fast against the shifters' tight, bony grip. The name rang in my ears, that was my name, that was me, and for the first time it sounded wonderful.

"So," Freya said. "Let's get what I brought you here for."

In my daze, I almost didn't notice Freya reach out for me. Her fingers looked like talons, and for a moment I saw what she really was underneath the make up and glossy hair, under the thin membrane of skin. She was insane.

Nick flew at her, and beat her to the ground. She retaliated with a kick to his jaw, and more shifters appeared to hold him back as she grabbed me again.

I was on the floor, at some point I had sank to my knees, and she straddled me, pinning me to the floor. She pushed down on my arms, and pain shot through my elbows to my shoulders. *Come on, don't just lay there! She's going to break your arms!*

I heaved her off me with a huge effort that made me feel sick, and I pushed her roughly to the ground. I tried to gather the energy, but it was too far away. It was as though it had been sucked right out of existence.

Freya punched me hard in the face, with a force that shocked me. She glared at me with fire beneath her eyes. Her hair was out of place, her dress was torn. She spat at me. The blood that came out of her mouth was red.

She clicked her fingers, and two shifters brought in two people I had hoped would remain out of this fight: Ash and Beth.

They shuffled out, their skin a grey, ill colour, their eyes white. My heart broke in that instant.

"Oh God," I whispered. "Please give them back to me, please."

"They are mine now, you stupid bitch," she said. "Now either you play nice, or I start snapping necks."

I glanced at Nick, but he only looked back at me helplessly. He had killed several of the shifters that had been holding him back, but they kept coming, they were endless.

If there was nothing more that could be done for them, then why was she using Ash and Beth as leverage? A part of them must be there, inside. They weren't completely gone, not just yet. I ran to them and fell at their feet. I took each of their hands, stopping for only a second to think about how cold they were.

"Please, please forgive me. I'm so sorry, I'm sorry…please…" They didn't move, didn't acknowledge me at all. "God, snap out of it! Please! We can go home and it will all be over."

Freya had kidnapped them at some point, that much I knew. I

knew their friendship wasn't fake, I felt it, I had felt loved and wanted. They were genuine people, it was real. *But how long have they been here?*

I didn't see Freya creep up behind them. Maybe it had been her plan all along, maybe I didn't take her seriously enough. She touched Beth's throat, almost delicately, between her hands. I opened my mouth to scream, but Freya snapped her neck like a twig before I could make a sound.

I remember screaming, I remember grabbing Beth as she fell. The rest is a strange, hazy blank. No one else in the world existed then, apart from me and my wonderful, selfless friend. Her eyes closed, and as they did, a single milky tear fell from her right eye. She was smiling.

I cradled her head on my knees. I rocked, I kissed her forehead. I called her name over and over. Freya came to sit beside me. Her breath was hot on my neck. I wanted to kill her, to make her suffer, to make her hurt more than anyone had ever hurt before, but I couldn't risk losing Ash too.

"I said play nice," she whispered to me. "Now, what do you say?"

What else could I do? I had to give myself up, to save Ash. It was the least I could do after everything I had caused.

"Jenny! No! She'll kill us all anyway! Jenny!" It was Nick, somewhere in the background, far away. He was muffled, or maybe it was my ears.

"Will you let them go?" I asked. "If I give myself up?"

"Yes, my dear. Of course," Freya said. She was lying. We both knew it. But I wasn't strong enough to take her on. It might give Ash and Nick a few extra seconds to get away.

"Okay, just do it," I said.

She smiled at me, she was victorious now. I forced myself to keep my eyes open as she reached out to me. I needed to see my own fate, and not be a coward anymore. But her hand froze in mid air, and she started to shriek. Once, then again, and again.

It was the most horrific thing I had ever heard.

CHAPTER FORTY-THREE

Ash

I thought of nothing, everything was white, I couldn't see properly. I was so cold, freezing; I couldn't get warm. My heart thudded in my chest painfully, and my lungs ached for fresh air.

How long have I been like this?

It felt like a lifetime of no control, of no free will. Everything I saw seemed far away, out of my reach, I was screaming inside, for someone to help me, but no words came out. My mouth couldn't even open. I felt no hunger, no thirst, it was as if I was dead, but something had inhabited my body and was walking around, wearing it.

I could feel Beth next to me, she was still here, still alive, but I couldn't turn my head to look at her, I couldn't hold her, comfort her, tell her it will be okay.

From the day those things took us, the day we went to Lincoln, I had wondered what we had done to deserve this, why it was us they had taken, us they had locked up, us they had poisoned so we would become one of them. But then that woman started questioning us about Aria, about how we knew her, and where she was and what she had told us. But we couldn't tell her what she wanted to hear, so we were punished.

I don't know how many times they had tried to get information out of us that we just couldn't give them, but when they last questioned Beth, I heard her horrific screams from down the corridor, and it made me vomit so intensely that I had passed out.

I had a rage inside me I had never felt before, but they were too strong, and this thing controlling me was taking me over more and more each day. I felt it growing inside me, overwhelming my body and my mind. It was eating up my soul, taking me as its prisoner. I was powerless.

Thinking about all the things I had yet to do with my life saved me from total darkness. I wanted to go to University to study art, hopefully one day set up my own gallery. Go places, travel, meet a girl, get married, have children, grandchildren. My life that had always stretched out before me, with years to spare, had suddenly come to a halt. I kept wondering whether this day would be my last, when the urge to give in would be too great, and I would let go, and cease to exist. I prayed to God I wouldn't die, I prayed every day.

As I stood there, helplessly watching as one of my best friends tried one last time to reach me, to reach Beth, and I couldn't even return her gaze. *I'm here! I'm here!* I wanted to shout. But my jaw clenched shut, and my body felt numb. Aria took my hand, and I could feel how warm and full of life she was, and she tried, so hard, she tried.

She then let go, but I was left with something, a small surge of energy. It was small and light, yet powerful. It flowed through me, slowly, as if it had trouble getting around, and eventually it reached my heart. It was as though something had been awakened, released, and I felt a strange power wash over me. It was my ability; I felt it, inside. It was ready, alive, and it wanted payback.

But I was too late, and I stood by motionless, as Beth was killed. Everything left me then, I wanted to die with her, I wanted to just disappear. Anger against Aria rose inside me; this was her fault, she had put us in danger. But now Freya was going to kill her too, and even if this was Aria's fault, I had to do something.

I was extremely shaky at the best of times, but I concentrated, and looked that evil bitch right in the face. I wanted her to hurt, to writhe in agony. I wanted to boil her blood in her veins, to sizzle her brain in its own juices. Would it work? I felt the power grow inside me, stronger, and I reached out with my mind, to Freya, and touched her. I channelled all my anger, frustration, fear, horror, hopelessness, and I felt that familiar push, the urgency, and I let it go, all of it.

CHAPTER FORTY-FOUR

Jenny

Freya clutched the sides of her head, and screamed and writhed around on the floor. I stood up in shock, my eyes glued to the scene in front of me. Red marks appeared on her skin. They looked like burns. She saw me try and move away, and reached out for me, but the skin on her fingers blistered, peeled away, and I kicked free of her grasp, pulling off parts of her skin in the process.

What the fuck is going on?

I looked around me, trying to bite back the terror I felt inside, and my eyes landed on Ash. He was still under Freya's spell, but his eyes, they were burning, the heat, the intensity, I had never seen anything like the fury I saw in him then. I looked back at Freya. Her skin had melted away, her hair fell to the floor in clumps. She screamed again, and again, and then let out a sob of such pain that I immediately wanted it to be over. I didn't enjoy standing there watching such agony.

"Ash!" I warned. I needed him to hurry up. But he didn't. He ignored me, and carried on his slow torture until there was nothing left of Freya but a pile of charred bones.

As Freya lay smouldering on the floor, all around us the shapeshifters fell to their knees, and disintegrated into blue puddles. Ash collapsed, and I ran over to him.

"Ash! Oh God! Ash!" I grabbed him to try and break his fall, and I laid him down. I shook him, but then soon stopped when

I realised what state he was in. He was beaten badly, with bruises and cuts peppering his skin. I didn't dare to check the rest of him.

Nick's solid frame was soon lifting Ash up onto his shoulders.

"I need to get him to a hospital," he said.

Beth's body was still lying there. She looked so small, lonely. I had dared to hope for a second that perhaps she would come to life again, that now Freya was gone, she'd be okay. But it doesn't work like that. Although, I couldn't just leave her there, in this dungeon, this place of such darkness.

"Can you help me with Beth?" I asked.

He looked at her for a moment; if it was up to him, we would leave her here, she was dead after all, but he knew that I wouldn't let that happen.

"Sure thing."

He took Ash outside and came back soon after for Beth. He held her close to him as they meandered through the rooms of this cave, and I followed behind, unable to take my eyes off her. I couldn't help but notice the subtle but alarming difference between holding someone in your arms who was unconscious, and holding someone who was dead. The life had truly been ripped away from her, everything that made her Beth, and she was left with an empty casing. I thought back then to the night that all this started, the night I showed my cowardice for what it was, and I knew that all this mess, all these people who had died, was all my fault. I'd asked Laura to take away my responsibility, and all it did was come back with a vengeance and remind me that nobody can hide.

Nick laid Beth down on the grass a few yards from the opening of Freya's prison, next to Ash. I placed my hands on her slim, pale frame, still warm.

"What are you doing?" Nick asked.

It must have been early evening, and the sun was low in the sky, yet its rays were still glowing through the trees. I did this final thing for my friend. I hated that it was such a beautiful sunset; she would have loved it.

I ran my fingers across her face one last time, trying to memorise her long brown hair, her large eyes, her full lips and her friendly, warm smile. I couldn't bear the thought of waking up one day and realising that I couldn't remember some part of her that I used to. I tried to remember everything, in that moment. Then, I was ready.

"I'm returning her to the earth," I replied. I kissed her cheek. I then closed my eyes, and I asked for Beth's body to be returned to the ground, to be returned to the energy that once gave her life. The energy took her, and her skin shone a brilliant, glittering green before her body disappeared.

Nick called for an ambulance, and we met the paramedics at the edge of the woods. I rode with Ash in the back. The paramedics asked me questions about what had happened. What could I say? I said he'd been attacked my a group of thugs. One of the guys whistled through his teeth, and said "not half; this guy's a mess." *Please don't, I already know, just make him better, please.*

They took Ash into a private room, and I was told I had to wait in the reception area. Nick met me there. When I saw him, he took me in his arms and held me as I sobbed.

We sat there for hours, I don't know how long, and Nick brought me food, coffee, water, but I was in a kind of stasis, a catatonic stupor. I didn't dare to move, I didn't dare to think, not until I knew Ash was okay.

Nick was quiet, helpful, reserved, but I knew he had questions.

These would have to come later. I couldn't deal with telling him anything now. I just didn't have the strength.

Finally, we were allowed to see Ash. The state of him hit me when I saw him lying in that bed. I was told that one of his arms was broken, so were several ribs. He had internal bleeding, a shattered eye socket, and external injuries that looked like someone had carved into him with a knife.

With shaking hands, I reached out and stroked his hair. He was unconscious, or asleep, I wasn't sure which. But upon my touch, he winced, and then groaned, and then his eyes flashed open. He didn't see me. Instead, he saw something that no one else did, right ahead of him, and he started to scream. He screamed and screamed until the nurses gave him something to calm him down. He went back to sleep, and Nick led me away.

We went back around an hour later. Ash was awake, he was lucid, and he was looking out of the window. I was overwhelmed with relief, but I also knew what was coming, before it was said.

"Get out," he whispered to me.

"Ash, I…"

"Get away from me." He turned around slowly to face me.

"Ash…please, I need to explain…"

"You ruined my life. I never want to see you again."

And so I left, in a daze. Nick drove me home, and I sat down heavily on the sofa, and cried in the way that only people who have lost everything, who have nothing to live for, have cried. I yelled and fought against Nick as he tried to calm me down. I ripped at my clothes, my hair, I screamed until my voice was hoarse. But nothing would make this guilt go away. It was like something was inside, eating away.

CHAPTER FORTY-FIVE

Carl

I tried to concentrate on my morning newspaper, attempting to distract myself with it. My untouched cup of tea sat on the coffee table, getting cold. My reading glasses slipped from my nose, and I pushed them back in frustration. The words in front of me were gibberish; I was reading the same line over and over. Nothing was going in.

I threw the newspaper down, and gazed around the living room. Margaret had always kept the house spotless, taking pride in it, showing it off when we had guests round. She was always a very proud, sensible woman, but also a passionate one. This passion shone through during the years she brought up our three children. She doted on them all, spoiling them, buying them anything they wanted.

Of course, they have all grown up now, but Margaret still maintained a hard, fierce love for them even when they weren't here. When she knew they were coming round for dinner, she would spend the whole day cleaning the house from top to bottom, and dusting the unused furniture, books and other belongings the children still kept in their old rooms. I wasn't sure if it was them or Margaret who never wanted to throw their old stuff away, but then I never knew much about what went on around here. I was always at work, looking after other people's children better than I looked after my own. I was absent from them, disconnected, the long hours at the facility making me miss a large portion of their childhood. But they never resented me, they knew the work I did and how important it was. Margaret, however, sometimes grew frustrated at the fact I was missing my children grow up.

"They'll be gone, one day, you know," she used to say. "You'll miss them more than they'll miss you." She was right, but what could I do? My work always came first. My colleagues were my only friends, my other family. The fights Margaret and I used to have about it, she would accuse me of abandoning my family for my employees, that it wasn't healthy.

When I finally retired, I could tell how relieved she was, but she had seen me deteriorate, and we both knew it was only a matter of time, the calm before the storm. When the storm hit, it poisoned a good portion of my lungs, and Margaret's time was then spent caring for me.

During the chemotherapy she dressed, bathed and fed me, and I felt ridiculous for it. That's when the housework suffered, and for the first time in out forty-year marriage, Margaret left the house to its own devices, collecting dust, becoming musty. All my life she came second, or even third, to my work and my children, but I was always her number one priority, I was her life. I loved this woman with all my heart, and only when I grew old, and I was told I had six months to live, did I realise what I had missed. I started appreciating her, seeing her how I should have always seen her. She was a saint, and I didn't deserve her, or the love she showed me.

The chemotherapy sessions finally ceased, and I had to admit I wasn't getting any better. I was dying, wasting away, before my own eyes. Since then I have merely been existing, the days and weeks slipping away, knowing the inevitability of my death sentence, the moment I cease to exist becoming ever-more real.

I could almost taste it. And this is my reward, to die unbearably slowly, as an old, frail man, everybody feeling sorry for me.

This is my comeuppance, my punishment, for what happened at the facility. I was the boss, the person in charge, I had years of experience behind me, and everyone looked to me for advice. A fire, of all things. Those poor, poor people. And Laura; my good friend and work colleague, I am sorry I left you on your own without support. I should have been there more. Dying isn't an excuse to become lazy, after all.

After I heard about that tragic evening, I'm not sure if it was the cancer, or the panic, perhaps it was both, but I was admitted to hospital. Those weeks were a blur. I had only been back a day or so when Margaret handed me my mail. My hands landed shakily on a letter addressed to someone else, in Laura's handwriting. I knew she was alive – even in my half conscious state at the hospital I had had that checked into – but would she ever talk to me again? Would she blame me for everything?

I stood up, my bones aching, and with Margaret's help I got dressed, and I was out the door, clutching the letter in my hands.

CHAPTER FORTY-SIX

Jenny

I am alone, it is dark, I try desperately to see in front of me, but there is nothing. I stretch out my hand, and I exclaim when I cannot even see it. Have I gone blind? I wonder in panic. What's happening? I walk forwards and then back again, and all around, holding my arms outstretched, trying to find a wall or a door. I find nothing, and slump to the ground in fear and frustration. I then see a light, small at first, to my left, like a candle or a lamp. As I turn, I gasp in horror as the light becomes bigger.

It is hot white, burning my eyes. I back away, but it follows. It gets larger and larger, until it is almost the size of a person, and that's when it took its shape. The light swirled and twisted itself, forming arms, legs, torso, a face. Beautiful red hair, bright blue eyes.

It was Laura. She smiled warmly at me, and knelt down so she and I were at eye level. My breath caught in my throat, and my body felt weak. I flinched as she reached out to touch me, to stroke my face. I couldn't see what she was wearing, the aura around her shone too brightly.

"Hush," she whispered, her brow furrowing in concern. "It's okay."

"What's happening?" I asked, trying to squirm away. She took my hand in hers, and searched my eyes. I tried to steady my pounding heart, but it thumped hard in my chest. My hand became clammy, and I felt sweat creeping up my back.

She said nothing to console me, only pulled me closer to her, and I sighed heavily, realising how much I missed her. She smelt the way she used to smell, powdery and fresh, and I felt her heart beating against my ear. Her slender, pale hand pushed back my hair gently, and I closed my eyes. She whispered into my ear, low and slight, almost as though she hadn't said anything at all.

"I'm sorry, baby." I almost didn't hear her, but her words rang in my ears.

I heard her say it again.

"I'm sorry, baby."

She held me tight, and I held her, and I cried, hard. I sobbed, my tears falling onto her. I then pulled away from her, and her eyes met mine. They were wet, full of sorrow.

"It's okay," I managed to whisper, "It's okay." I wiped my eyes, and tried to steady myself.

"You have to wake up now," she said, and I panicked.

"No," I replied, my hands gripping her tighter.

"Yes," she said, as she took my shaking hands and held them between hers.

"But when I wake up, you won't be there." I didn't want to lose her again; I wanted to hold on, to stay.

"I'll be there," she said, smiling softly. "Don't you worry about that."

I woke up drenched in sweat. A dream. I sighed, wiped away my tears. *You deserve to be haunted like this, don't moan about it. Take your poison.* I got out of bed.

I ended up spending the next few hours wandering around the house like a madwoman. I was collecting memories, memories of knick-knacks, ornaments, photos, clothes, furniture, it all hit me like a barrage of pain, of a life that I could never go back to. A pen that Nick had given me before we started dating, the dress

I wore the night we made love for the first time. Laura's favourite chair, her clothes, her make up, the smell of her hairspray, the book left on her nightstand, half-finished. I had bought her that book. It was a new one by her favourite author. It suddenly hit me that she never got a chance to finish it, and although it was a small thing, it brought out fresh tears and a new wave of grief.

I had never known my father, and Laura, who I had never really called "mum," brought me up by herself. She was a career woman, and I think deep down I wasn't really planned for, but she did an amazing job, and when I expressed an interest in working for her at the facility, she jumped at the chance to merge both her loves in one place.

Why didn't she tell me about the creatures? How could she not have told me about when they came for me as a child? Had she known about Freya? Why had they left it so long before coming for me again? There was so much I didn't know, and so much I would never know.

I thought about Beth, and how much she must have suffered because of me. Judging from Ash's injuries, I had wildly underestimated the extent of Freya's insanity. Who exactly was she? I wondered if Ash would ever speak to me again. Probably not. I didn't blame him.

There was a knock at the door. I shuddered in fright. I couldn't see anyone, I didn't have the strength. What if the shifters were back?

Nick opened the door, and standing there, small yet noble, wise, was a man that, in my old life, I had loved dearly.

"Carl," I said.

"Hello, dear."

CHAPTER FORTY-SEVEN

Jenny

Carl sat down heavily on the sofa. I sat down next to him and we hugged tightly. Nick brought in some tea and biscuits. I had always looked up to Carl, when he ran the facility he never forgot the main focus: the people. We were there to help those people. I grew up thinking of him as a granddad to me. He was always warm, caring, but at the same time he knew how to run the facility with ruthlessness. He was a no-nonsense, commanding director. He'd left Laura in charge about a year ago, early retirement I had thought, but it was clear now that he wasn't well, not at all.

"I'm so sorry about what happened, my dear," he said. "The facility, your mother, everything. My deepest sympathies."

I didn't know quite how to respond, so I just said thank you. How much does he know about what actually happened? Nick sat on the chair opposite us.

"I tried to contact you," he said. "When did you hear about the facility?"

Carl smiled sadly at us.

"I came to apologise. You see, I was given this." He produced a letter from his inside coat pocket. "It was delivered a few days after the accident. But…well, I haven't been home recently. The cancer, you see…it keeps me in hospital a lot. Well, Margaret gave me all my mail when I returned home the other day, and…this one wasn't addressed to me."

I saw the name on the envelope. It was for me. The handwriting, it was from Laura. My heart pounded in my ribcage.

"This is for you, my dear." He gave me the envelope, and I took it with shaking fingers. "I do apologise for the delay. Your mother was a fine woman, someone who I dearly miss. But you have her strength, and her determination, you must keep that with you at all times."

"Thank you," I said.

"Another thing," Carl continued. "Since the fire at the facility was regarded as accidental, there is some insurance coming to me. When it arrives, I would like to give you both a percentage, as an apology to you both for not giving you a safe working environment."

Does he really not know what actually happened?

"Carl, no, really, it's okay…" Nick tried to say.

"Don't be silly, it's the least I can do. It really is…" He paused then, and I knew what he was thinking. The poor souls that had died the night of the "fire." He had a lot of amends to make. He continued.

"It's the least I can do. Please accept it."

"Thank you, Carl," I said. I took his warm, slightly rough hand in mine. "But it was an accident, nothing to do with you."

"I should have kept a closer eye on it."

"Don't blame yourself," I whispered. *Blame me, it's my fault.*

"Anyway, I must be off. My taxi is waiting outside," he said. *Oh. I didn't realise this was only a fleeting visit. There's so much more to talk about.*

"You must both come over to the house sometime, it would be nice to see you," he said.

"Of course," I replied.

He got up with some effort, and I helped him to the door.

"Carl." I touched his arm. He'd lost weight. "I'm sorry about the cancer. I didn't know."

"It's quite alright, dear," he replied. "But you might want to come and visit sooner rather than later."

He smiled wistfully, and I couldn't help letting a pitiful half-sob escape my throat. Nick slipped his arms around my waist as we waved Carl goodbye.

We closed the door. Nick led me back to the sofa. The envelope was lying on the coffee table. It was too heavy for me to pick up at the moment.

"Jenny," Nick said. "I know this is tough, but if you need me… in any way…I'm here."

What?

"What do you mean?" I asked. "I need you all the time. I need you Nick. Why? What's wrong?"

"Well, I don't know. Everything's different now, we're different. I didn't know if you still…wanted me? I will understand if you need space."

"Why are you saying this to me? Nick, you're the only thing keeping me going. Everyone I know is dead, or dying, or not talking to me. If you left, I…don't know what I would do."

"Okay, I'm sorry."

"Do you…do you want to leave?"

I thought then, for the first time, that this might all be too much for him. He wrapped his arms around me.

"No, I'm sorry I brought it up. I just want you to be okay."

I laughed bitterly. "I'm not sure I remember how that feels."

"Do you want to open the letter?"

"Not now."

"Okay."

"Nick…I need to explain to you what happened that night."

"No you don't sweetie."

"I do."

"Jenny…"

"I asked Laura to take away my memory. Not all of it, just… she told me why the shifters had attacked the place. She had seen them before. They'd come for me before. They wanted my ability. For Freya. But I'm a coward. I couldn't bear that fact that I had caused something so horrific. I chose to hide, instead of giving myself over to them. I was a selfish, spoilt, childish coward. Laura took away what she had just confessed, but then a shifter killed her, leaving the rest of my memory to be eaten away too. I caused everything. If only I had been brave, and faced up to my responsibilities."

"It's alright, Jenny. You don't have to explain yourself to me. I've done things recently that I've not been proud of…torturing those poor people trapped in the shifters…but its done, in the past. And I'll love you all the same, for the rest of my life. There's nothing that will change that."

Don't be so sure about that, a voice inside me said.

Don't be so sure, darling.

CHAPTER FORTY-EIGHT

Jenny

That evening, I was sitting pensively on one of the branches of the willow tree. It had been a while since I had visited her, a lifetime, and it felt nice to feel her against me. Sparks of energy hung from her leaves, dripped from her trunk, it was exquisite. She held my frame as I read the letter from Laura.

It was written on the afternoon of the fire, after Nick had come to her with a vision that the shifters were coming, only at the time he didn't know what they were. I don't think she ever knew about Freya.

She wrote the letter after sending out the message to evacuate. The letter itself was short, scrawled. She had written it quickly. It was mostly an apology, a plea for forgiveness, and an explanation of everything that I now already knew. *Laura, how could you have been so secretive?*

She told me she loved me, and she would explain more when we got out. Maybe part of her knew she wouldn't though. Why else would she write this? I wondered then how she had posted it. She must have had to run to the postbox at the end of the road, and then come back. She could have escaped at that point, she could have just walked away with her life. How brave of her, to go back into the gates of hell, and try and fight her way through.

I had decided I was going to see Ash again tomorrow, even if he didn't want to see me. I needed to explain, to let him know I was here for him. He saved us all really. He killed Freya.

I can't be killed dear. I can only hide. I hid deep this time, to escape my confines.

I closed my eyes. Was I going crazy? Was this voice a consequence of my guilt? Of my poor choices? She came and she went, she mostly spoke when I tried to sleep. Maybe it was my comeuppance, maybe it was exactly what I deserved.

It's not so bad, darling. Not so bad at all.

Laura

He came through the window. He pinned me down to the bed, forced himself inside, into a place I had never let anyone go before. He smelt of something old...I couldn't put my finger on it. His bald head shone in the moonlight, his black coat flapped against the breeze. I could shout, scream, call the police, but they would never catch him, I knew that much. It had been so long since he had been human.

It was over quickly, at least. He was still lying over me as he whispered into my ear.

"I'll be back for her."

I was too shocked, too frightened to say anything back. But as he got up, composed himself once again and disappeared back out of the window, a thought repeated itself in my head.

No you won't; she's mine. She's mine and you won't take her from me.

ABOUT THE AUTHOR

Bekki Pate was born and raised in Nottingham, but currently lives in Cannock with her partner. She works in clinical trials for oncology within the NHS, and in her spare time she is an avid reader. She tries to read a wide variety of books, from horror to romance, but her favourite author is Stephen King; whom she considers to be an absolute genius. She enjoys having the famous Cannock Chase right next door; as it's where she goes for a bit of peace and quiet, as well as inspiration for new stories.